Sabotage
Copyright © 2022 by Shantel Tessier
All rights reserved.

For more information about the author and her books, visit her website— https://shanteltessier.com/
You can join her reader group. It's the only place to get exclusive teasers, first to know about current projects and release dates. And also have chances to win some amazing giveaways- https://www.facebook.com/groups/TheSinfulSide

Editor: Amanda Rash & Jenny Sims
Formatter: Christina Parker Smith
Cover and interior designer: Melissa Cunningham

PLAYLIST

"Joke's On You" by Charlotte Lawrence
"Bad Moon" by Hollywood Undead
"In The End" by Black Veil Brides
"vicious" by Tate McRae
"Middle Of The Night" by Elley Duhé

WARNING

For those of you who wish to go in blind; please remember this dark romance is a work of fiction, and I do NOT condone any situations or actions that take place between these characters. Continue to the prologue, just remember that I warned you. If you do NOT want to go in blind: please read the trigger warnings listed below.

AUTHOR'S NOTE:

Nothing about this is to be taken seriously. It is strictly a work of fiction and for your smut pleasure.

Sabotage may contain triggers for some. If you've never read a dark romance, please don't start with this one.

Trigger Warnings include:

rape, branding/cutting, sexual torture, graphic violence, drug/alcohol use.

If you have any questions, feel free to email me, and one of my assistants or I will get back to you. shanteltessierassistant@gmail.com

Some things to know about Sabotage

It is not an RH

It is MF with an MFMM scene (no MM interaction, they are focused on her)

The h ends up with one H

It is told in multiple POVs

OTT (over the top) H

J/P (jealous and possessive) H

A Dark College/Stepbrother Romance

One thing you need to know about me—is that I'm not you. Once you understand that, this will make more sense. – **Raylee** (ray-LEE)

USA TODAY & WALL STREET JOURNAL BESTSELLING AUTHOR

SHANTEL TESSIER

Prologue

COLTON

"GODDAMN." I GROAN at the feel of the woman on her knees. My hands tighten in her bleach blond hair, and I suck in a deep breath while my hips lift on their own off the dining room chair where I'm sitting.

My breathing picks up, and the sound of her sucking on my cock fills the formal dining room. She doesn't gag very often. No, I've trained my little slut very well.

Opening my eyes, I look down into her crystal blue ones, and they're drowning in tears as she stares up at me. Some are already running down her cheeks, smearing her makeup that she painted on before she went out earlier tonight. She may have danced and flirted with other men, but I knew she'd come home to me—she always does—needing to be fucked.

That's one of the reasons I forced her to live with me. I've always got my eye on her.

Giving her hair a little tug, I pull her head off my cock, and she keeps her mouth open and ready for me to violate it some more. "Such a good girl." I groan, licking my lips.

A line of drool runs down her chin when she sticks her tongue out, waiting impatiently. Releasing her hair with my left hand, I shove three fingers into her mouth, forcing her head back. She blinks rapidly from the invasion as a wave of new tears runs down her pretty face. "You like that, don't you, princess?"

She tries to nod but can't, so instead, garbled words come from her.

"Yeah, a dirty slut loves having her mouth full." Removing my fingers, she sucks in a breath, and I slap her across the face, making her cry out. It wasn't hard enough to hurt, but it definitely stung. "Say it," I demand.

She shifts on her knees in her white clubbing dress. It dips low in the front, showing off her impressive tits, and is barely long enough to cover her pussy. I'm going to shred that thing before the night is over with. "Colt—"

I slap her again, cutting her off, and then grip her chin, my other hand still holding her by her hair. She whimpers, and I lean forward, my face inches from hers, and I spit into her mouth. "Say it, princess. Tell me that you're my good little slut, and that you'll do anything to please me."

Some women are stuck-up bitches who don't like to explore their sexuality. Raylee Lexington Adams isn't one of them. This woman is pure ecstasy. The fact that I hate her fucking guts makes this even better. Knowing she hates me just as much is icing on the cake.

We are hate sex at its finest.

"I'm your good little slut," she finally moans, shifting on her knees once again. "I'll do whatever you want."

I smile down at her.

"Please?" she begs. Her once red-painted lips are now smeared and open for me again, so I let go of her chin but keep the other in her hair.

"Prove it," I challenge, sitting back in my chair. Snickering comes from the men sitting around the dining room table to my right, but I ignore them.

Leaning forward, she wraps her lips around the head of my dick once again, and I shove her face down, holding my cock inside her mouth. She shifts on her knees, and I lift my hips again, going deeper. The tightness I feel once I slide down the back of her throat takes my breath away.

Fuck, I want to throw her on her back and fuck her face until I'm coming all over it. But I can't. Not tonight. I knew she'd come home wet and ready for me. I had a plan. One that will come in handy eventually. I'm all about playing games. Raylee and I have been playing them for years. And I learned very quickly that the only way to win against her is to play the long game.

Releasing her hair, I lift my hands and lock my fingers behind my head, relaxing into my chair while she gasps and spits all over my dick. She looks up at me through watery and matted mascara-coated lashes. A look of utter desperation in her gorgeous blue eyes.

Fuck, she's absolutely stunning.

My teeth grind at that thought. I hate that about her. How she parades around town with other men. How she knows what to wear to turn me on. And the fact that I can smell her in this house. It's aggravating, to say the least. I hate this bitch with everything inside me, but even I can't deny that I want her. That's what makes this so much worse. That I can't get enough of her.

"I'm not convinced, princess," I inform her, making a tsking sound with my tongue and teeth.

Her wrists are tied behind her back with my belt so she can't use her hands. She's going to have to show me what her mouth can do. As if I don't already know.

Her eyes narrow up at me, making them darken, and she bares her perfectly straight white teeth. Good. I want her angry. Because I'm going to humble her real soon.

Laughter grows from the guys to my right, but we both ignore them. She doesn't care who watches as long as she gets what she wants. Plus, she's into humiliation and degradation. They turn this slut on.

Taking in a long breath, she lowers her open mouth to my cock and swallows me whole. Her anger making her more determined than ever to get me off. Just another level of our game that she doesn't have a chance at winning. I lean my head back and close my eyes like before, enjoying how good her hot and wet mouth feels.

Soon, I feel my balls tighten, and I look down to watch. Her head bobs fast, and I'm about to explode down her throat.

With every ounce of willpower I have, I shove her off me. She sprawls onto the floor on her side, and I grip my dick just as I come. Some gets on my jeans, but most of it covers the black marble floor next to her.

I take in a few deep, calming breaths just watching her lie there. She's gasping, eyes closed, hands still restrained behind her back. Her white party dress has ridden up around her waist, showing me the lace, nude-colored thong that is high up on her hip. I bet if I spread her legs, they'd be soaking wet. Opening her eyes, she pulls her knees up and manages to tuck them underneath her so she can sit up.

I reach out, pushing her matted hair away from her wet face, tucking it behind her ear, allowing her to see. "Look at the mess you made," I say, pointing at the cum covering the floor in front of her.

She whimpers, her body shaking with need. My princess wants more. A slut is never satisfied.

Leaning forward, I wrap my free hand around her slender neck, feeling her pulse race, and gently kiss the side of her face. She tastes like the ocean—salty—from all the tears she's cried, and I whisper, "Clean it up."

Her body trembles while she breathes my name. "Colt—"

"Clean it up!" I order, standing from the chair. I grip her hair and shove her face-first onto the floor next to the cum.

She cries out but then wiggles her body to lie in a more comfortable position, flat on her stomach.

I shift my legs to where I'm standing over her, one boot on either side of her ass that is now showing thanks to her dress. "That's what sluts do, princess," I tell her, holding the side of her face to the cold floor while she sniffs. "They clean up their messes. And you're my good little slut, right?"

She nods the best she can and sucks in a breath.

"Say it."

"I'm-I'm your good little slut," she whispers, spit flying from her mouth.

"Now, show me."

She parts her lips, and her tongue darts out, licking at the cum, smearing it across the floor.

"Good girl," I praise her, and she whimpers. I let go of her hair and smooth it away from her face. "All of it, princess. Every drop. Clean up your mess."

I take a few steps back and look down at her. She's rocking from side to side, her arms fighting being restrained by my belt, with her tongue stretched out as far as it'll go to lick up the cum, and I smile. Every time I have her like this, it's a small victory.

Getting an idea, I bend over, grip her thighs, and shove them apart. Then I fall to my knees between them on the floor. "I knew it." Smiling, I look over the wet spot on her nude underwear. Since her legs are spread, she's got her ass tilted up off the floor to give me a great view.

I move the thong to the side and run my knuckles over her wet cunt, my mouth watering for a taste. She's completely shaved. I know she did this thinking she'd get lucky tonight.

"Please?" she begs. The desperation in her voice makes me want to cave and bury my face between her legs to eat her out right here while she licks my cum up off the floor. But I don't because this is what she does. She's my slut, not the other way around.

I slap her ass hard enough to leave a red handprint. She cries out and tries to get away from me, but there's nowhere for her to go. "Did I tell you that you were done?" I ask, my palm now rubbing her ass and my fingers digging into the sensitive skin.

Her body shakes, but I hear her softly answer. "No."

"Then keep licking," I command. "I want that floor clean, princess."

I ignore her soft cries as she goes back to what she was doing while my eyes drop back to her pussy. I can't help myself; I shove a finger into her and bite my tongue to keep from groaning out loud over how wet she is. Don't want her to hear how much I want her.

Removing it, I stick it in my mouth. "Desperation tastes so good," I say, pulling it free from my lips.

The boys laugh at the table, and this time, I look over at them. They each sit in their chairs, pushed back from the table to allow them the best view of her. Finn has a joint between his lips, one hand holding the handle of his knife while he twirls the end of the blade against his other palm, watching her lick up my cum. Alex is smoking a cigarette, his eyes glued to her ass up in the air. And Jenks, well, he's doing what I told him to do. I wait for him to make eye contact, and then I nod at him. He does the same before pocketing his cell.

Looking back down at her glistening cunt, I thrust two fingers into her this time, making her moan. I know she wants more. Raylee likes it rough. I start to fuck her with my fingers, her body rocking back and forth. She whimpers and gasps between sounds of her tongue lapping at the floor like an addict who spilled what little drug she had left and won't let it go to waste.

Her pussy clamps down on my fingers, and I feel her body stiffen. I remove them, and her body sags the best it can in her position while her panting now fills the silent room. I like to tease her. Make her crawl on her hands and knees while begging for me to fuck her.

I look down at the floor and see that she has cleaned up most of what I gave her. "Good girl." I smile.

Standing, I grip her bleach blond hair. I yank her to her feet, and she cries out before I toss her onto her back on the formal dining room table, crushing her arms underneath her, making her scream this time.

"Finn, shut her up," I tell him.

He stands from the chair and removes his belt. "Open wide." Before she has a chance to follow orders, he's placing his belt into her mouth, shoving it behind her teeth, and then wrapping it around her head. He ties it off, securing it in place.

I lean over the end of the table, reaching up and running my thumb over her teeth where she bites on the black leather. She's got cum on her face and in her hair from the floor. She breathes heavily through her nose. I grab the almost see-through material she calls a dress and rip it down the center, exposing her breasts. She isn't wearing a bra. I'm honestly surprised she was even wearing underwear.

Running my hands up her ribs, I grab her large breasts in my hands and squeeze, making her rock her body back and forth, rattling the table.

Her eyes go from mine to my three friends, and I watch them grow even heavier. I also notice her nipples harden, and she arches her neck. *Interesting.*

"Who wants a taste?" I ask.

I've never let them have a piece of her before. If I'm being honest with myself, I hate the fact that she fucks other men. But I can't let her know that about me. And this is about my control over her right now, not the other way around.

She's my fucking toy to use and pass around.

Finn leans down into her face, blowing out a puff of smoke from his joint. She rocks her head back and forth while unintelligible words come from her gagged mouth. Laughing, he answers, "I'd love a piece."

I lift her knees, placing her black hooker heels on the table, and push her upward so she's more in the center. "Spread your legs, princess," I order her, and they fall open. "Such a greedy slut." I slap her inner thigh, making a loud popping noise.

She arches her back and tries to relieve the pressure off her restrained arms pinned underneath her, but Alex places his hands around her neck, holding her in place at the other end of the table.

I rip her underwear off and shove a finger into her. Pulling it out, I hold it up in front of Finn's face. He parts his lips, and I push my finger into his mouth. When he closes his lips around it, his eyes grow heavy, and he moans from deep in his throat.

I pull it out and smile, making up my mind. "Remove the belt from her mouth."

Alex lets go of her neck and undoes the belt, yanking it from her mouth. Placing my hand under her neck, I lift her to sit up and bring her face to mine. She looks like she's been through a thunderstorm—tears, drool, and cum cover her face and hair. She looks fucking gorgeous.

"You missed some," I say as I run my finger along her wet cheek, cleaning off some of the cum and smearing it over her plump lips.

She licks them and then opens her mouth, waiting for me.

"Do you want to come?" I ask her, knowing she'd do anything for me to get off right now. I left her on the edge for a reason.

Nodding once, she begs, "Please," and starts to cry. "Colt, I need it. God please ..."

"Shh," I say, planting a soft kiss on her forehead and then bringing my eyes to hers again. "You belong to me tonight, understood?"

"But—"

"Let me make this very clear, princess." I grip her hair and yank her head back while I trail kisses along her jawline. "You are to please them. Only I please you. Understand?" They know how much I hate her, and they also know I'd kill them if they ever touched her behind my back. What can I say? I'm a complicated man.

I claimed her the moment I met her. And everyone in this town knows that. Another reason the men she goes after don't stay around for very long.

"And then I can come?" she asks, swallowing nervously.

I can't help but smile and drop my mouth to her exposed neck. "Depends."

"On what?" she whispers.

I pull back and meet her pretty, hopeful eyes. "If you're a good girl or not."

Licking her lips, she nods once. "Always."

"We'll see." Yanking on her hair, I pull her down onto the table and over to the edge on her side. I center her over the left corner with her back facing where I stand. That way, her ass and pussy hang off the edge of the table, and her head almost hangs off the other side. Easy access for all of them.

Finn already put his joint away and has his dick out. By the way he's looking at her mouth, I guess he's made up his mind where he's going.

Alex enters the formal dining room, and I didn't even realize he had left, but it's obvious by the canola oil in his hand, he's going to go for her ass.

Jenks is removing his shirt up and over his head and undoes his jeans before shoving them to his ankles, getting comfortable.

Leaning over her side, I grip the back of her knees and shove them up to her chest, locking them in place with my arm.

"Colt," she whimpers, her body trying to fight me. Her arms are still tied behind her back. I know she's uncomfortable. *Too bad.*

My free hand grabs her hair, and I yank it back, now completely off the side of the table. "Sluts don't get to choose how they're fucked, princess."

Alex and Jenks are placing condoms over their pierced dicks and stepping up to the head of the table to my right, where her ass and cunt hang off. Without any warning, Jenks starts fingering her pretty pink pussy, making her squirm more in my hands.

I lower my mouth to her lips and whisper, "They just take it. And you're my slut, aren't you?"

"Y—es," she cries out, and I don't have to look to know that Jenks is finger-fucking her.

Alex tosses the canola oil onto the center of the table, where it then rolls off onto the floor. "This might hurt." He laughs, and I watch him run his fingers over her ass, smearing the oil to get it ready. Once satisfied, he pushes one finger into her.

She moans, her body shaking against mine.

"Make them feel good." I lean down and kiss her cum-covered face. "You always make me feel so good, princess. It's their turn."

Her eyes close tightly, and she stiffens, her legs pushing up against my arm. "Relax, just relax and take it." Alex groans. "I know you like to have your ass fucked."

"Oh," she cries out. "God—"

Finn grabs her face and tilts her head up off the table while his free hand shoves two fingers into her mouth, shutting her up.

I look down at her pretty face, and tears run from her eyes like a waterfall. Could be because her body is twisted like a pretzel right now. It could be because she needs to get off. That'll have to wait.

Removing his fingers, he demands, "Open wide." She parts her lips for him before he guides his cock into her mouth.

Her body moves, rocking back and forth on the edge of the table. I'm bent over, holding her in place while my three best friends have their way with her. She gives me too much power over her. Stupid girl. She knows I'll only take advantage of it.

"I see why you fuck this slut even though you hate her." Alex groans. His cock slams in and out of her ass, not giving her much time to adjust. But he was right. His dick isn't the first one there. I was. And I wasn't easy on it.

"Right?" Jenks laughs, still fingering her. Waiting for Alex to be done with her ass so he can take his turn. With the position she's in, they can't both fuck her at the same time. "This cunt…" He bites on his lower lip. "She's so fucking wet." He pulls his fingers out and leans over, running his hand over the side of her face. "Feel how wet you are." He chuckles at himself. "But I'm not surprised. Sluts prefer to be used by multiple cocks at once."

She mumbles unintelligent noises around Finn's cock in her mouth while she blinks rapidly. I have the urge to lick it off her cheek but refrain. She'll be all mine later.

Finn whistles. "Shit, she's got a mouth on her." Shoving his cock all the way down her throat.

Her body shakes against the table, and her eyes grow heavy. "Don't you dare, Raylee," I growl, knowing exactly what's happening. I've trained her. "Don't you dare fucking come for them." Only I can please her. I didn't offer her up so she could get pleasure from them.

Finn drops his free hand to her face and pinches her nose, cutting off her air. Her eyes go wide, her body thrashing against all of us.

"I'm coming." Alex is the first to call out breathlessly. He slams into her ass one last time and grunts before pulling his semi-hard dick out and stepping back. He walks out of the formal dining room, removing his condom.

Jenks doesn't waste a second and grips her hip, slamming his dick inside her and not letting up. I watch and see her wetness coating his lower abdomen.

I'm surprised at the rage that bubbles up inside me, like a pot of water about to boil over. The thought of her coming all over his dick pisses me off. But I can't stop them now. She'll never let me live it down. This is what she expects from me. To be used. To be an object. We don't give a shit about one another.

"Fucckkkk." Finn growls, and then I watch him stiffen while he comes down her throat. When he pulls out, he lets go of her nose, and she's gasping for air as spit and cum fall out of the side of her mouth, landing on the table she's pinned to. "Good job, slut." He taps the side of her face before falling into a chair and all but passing out.

"Colt…" She cries my name. "I can't …"

"Raylee!" I warn. If she comes on Jenks's dick, I'm going to make her wish she hadn't. I'll beat that ass black and blue.

Jenks pulls out of her pussy, and she sags against the table and begins crying harder. "Turn her over," he orders.

I roll her from her side to her back, and he yanks her ass to the end of the edge where he stands. I move to stand where Finn was and lean over the side of the table, keeping her legs pinned to her chest. My head now right above hers. She looks up at me, tears rolling down her face, and I hear Jenks going back to fucking her.

"Please?" she begs. The single word is broken. "I need—"

"Do not fucking come, Raylee," I snap, more pissed off at myself than anything. I've fucked her enough to know that it takes quite a bit of effort to get her off. Who knew three dicks would do the trick?

"I can't stop it," she cries, now sobbing as fresh tears trail down the sides of her face. "Colt—"

I slap my free hand over her mouth and lower my face to the table to whisper in her ear. "If you come, I will tie you down and fuck you to the point you are about to come and then stop. Over and over. As many times as it takes for you to learn a lesson. Do you understand me?"

Her eyes start to roll back into her head, arching her neck, and just when I think she's about to disobey me and come all over Jenks's dick, he pulls out and stumbles back away from the table.

"Jesus, dude. We should just tie her to the table and use her all night." He licks his lips while his eyes scan over her.

Her pussy wasn't enough for him. I get it. It's never enough.

"You had your fun." I let go of her legs and slide my arms under her, picking her limp body up off the table. She lays semi-conscious across my arms while I carry her upstairs.

One

RAYLEE

I SIT IN the driver's seat of my car, parked outside of the house that I call a prison—three stories, white stucco, black shutters, wraparound porch, and multiple balconies with iron railings. Surrounded by the beautiful Pennsylvania woods, it looks like something you'd see on a TV show for the rich and famous. Makes me want to gag.

Cars litter the circle driveway because dipshit is throwing a party tonight. He didn't even ask if I cared, but I'm not surprised. It's his house. I just *get* to live here.

The lights from the dash illuminate the inside while "Joke's On You" by Charlotte Lawrence blares, the bass making my car rattle while I contemplate what most call love.

Do you ever get tired of being a woman? Don't you just want to know once what it feels like to be a man? To have a dick that can fuck whatever it wants and be slapped on the back for it, like you actually accomplished something?

Why can't women go crazy in their twenties and then want to settle down in their thirties and not be judged for it? If you're a virgin, you're too inexperienced, and they don't want to take the time to "teach" you. Yet if you've had multiple partners, then you've been used too much and aren't good enough for them.

These days, girls are being taught to raise the ceiling and break the glass. Be independent—you don't need a man. But I don't care how successful you are. People still need sex. Some kind of human interaction.

As a woman, I understand it. The need to use men but also believe in love. But society tells us to question that. With how high divorce rates are, you have to think—is there one person out there for you? Maybe that person is the one for you today, but what about in two years? Who says that the man you marry and have three children with won't fuck your best friend in your bed with your wedding pictures hanging on the wall while he tells her he won't leave you because of the kids? Then what?

I fucking kill him, that's what. Then I spend the rest of my life in prison while my mother raises my children, and they end up getting bullied because their mother is a murdering psycho who was once a whore back in her twenties.

Women will say things like; *it's just a man. You deserve better. Go out and find another one.* But why should I have to go and start over with someone else because he can't keep his dick in his pants? Why do I have to accept his betrayal? I wasn't raised to accept defeat. No. My mother raised me to fight fire with fire. Even if that means having to burn myself along with him.

I look out the windshield at the car parked in front of me. It's unique, rare. He ordered it after he graduated from college and went to work for his *daddy*. It's a black Lamborghini Sian and cost him a whopping 3.6 million dollars. I think it's ugly.

He's why I question everything. Men, love, sex. I'm where I'm at in my life because of him. The fucker has crossed the line. For years now, we've been going at it. I hate him. He hates me. It's what makes the world go round. I'm sure of it.

But the sex... Goddamn, it's off-the-charts amazing. That's what makes me so mad at myself and pissed off at the world. But just when one of us thinks we should stop, the other pulls us back in for another round. We both know it. Otherwise, I'm pretty sure we'd kill one another.

My mother married his father when we were in high school. Typical fairy-tale romance. She was a server who was overworked and underpaid. He was a billionaire who just so happened to walk in and sit in her section early one morning. Four months later, they were married. My stepdad is a nice guy. But my stepbrother? Let's just say he's a fucking nightmare. He was a year older than me, and I thought I would be free of him after he graduated high school. But nope. Once his father got me into Barrington University—an elite college for rich kids—he offered me a room in his house that he shares with his three best friends—like I was a stray dog that had nowhere to go. I had laughed, thinking it was some sick joke. My mother thought it was the best idea Colt ever had. She praises him and thinks he's the best thing to happen to us, other than his father, of course. I'll give it to him, he's good at being a stepson, but he lives to make my life miserable.

Looking at the clock on the dash, I see it's a quarter till midnight.

Now is as good a time as any. He's probably balls deep in some woman's mouth right now. One can only hope that I'm about to interrupt something so fun for him.

Throwing my long, bleach-blond hair over my left shoulder, I pick up the joint and lighter out of the cup holder, stuffing them into my bra for safekeeping. It's not to get high or to calm my nerves. It's from his personal stash that he thinks I don't know about.

My phone dings for the hundredth time in the past ten minutes, and I ignore it. The last time I checked, the video had over a million views in less than five hours. Instead, I dig into my purse and pull out my lipstick.

When I yank down my visor, the two lights on either side give me just enough visibility to reapply my Ruby Woo lipstick so it's fresh as can be. Smacking my red lips, I smile to myself, rubbing my teeth to make sure none got on them. Showtime.

Getting out of the car, I walk to my trunk and hear whispers from kids that linger outside of the house while "Bad Moon" by Hollywood Undead plays from the inside.

"Fuck," one guy hisses.

"Go get them," another orders.

I smile to myself. *Yes, go get them.* Not sure why they're so surprised to see me here. I fucking live here too. Do they expect me to go into hiding because of the video? If that's the case, then they don't know who I am. But they're about to find out.

I grab the metal baseball bat and small can of gasoline, not even bothering to shut the trunk. I'm not here to hide what I'm about to do.

As I walk over to his car, my mother's six-inch, red Christian Louboutin heels clap on the blacktop driveway. You gotta look your best when you decide to show your crazy. Otherwise, you're just another stupid bitch like all the rest. Any woman can allow a man to make her go insane. The point is to stand out—be remembered and feared for your toxicity—but look fuckable while you're doing it.

Coming to a stop at his car, I catch sight of some of the partygoers as they start running out the front double doors of the house as if there's a fire inside. I ignore them and set the five-gallon gas can on the ground, grip the bat, and swing it at the driver's side window.

"Fuck!" I hiss when it hits the glass and bounces back. My hands and arms vibrate from the motion, making them sting. This is harder than it looks. Removing one hand at a time, I try to shake them out.

"Oh my god, Ray. What the fuck are you doing?" I hear Tatum—my best friend—yelling while she runs down the front steps in a black mini-dress and Dior heels.

I could ask her *why the fuck she's at my house partying* when she told me she had other plans tonight when I offered to go out on a double date, but I don't. Instead, I stay on track. Widening my stance, I make sure to put all my weight on the balls of my feet. I'd hate to fall off the back of my heels. Gripping the bat tighter, I swing again. It bounces off this time as well.

"You—"

Sucking in a deep breath, I let out a scream, interrupting her, and swing the bat. This time, I aim for the edge, making it shatter. "Thank fuck." I sigh. That'd be pretty damn embarrassing if I couldn't get it done with an audience. I toss the bat to the side and reach inside the now broken window, being careful not to cut my arm, to unlock it with a laugh. "Look at that." It was already unlocked. Of course, the motherfucker wouldn't have his car locked because no one would ever fuck with his shit.

I could have checked first, but if you ask anyone who knows me, they'll tell you that I can be dramatic. Plus, I just like to break shit. It can be very therapeutic.

When I pop the door open, the broken glass falls at my feet, and my heels crush it while I pick up the gas can. Looking inside, seeing the shattered glass covering the black and gray seats and floor makes me smile. Unscrewing the lid, I reach in and start shaking the can, letting the gas sprinkle all over. I don't really think there's a right or wrong way to do it. It's not like I googled it or anything. I'm just going by what feels natural.

Then I think *what the hell* and toss the entire thing into the car.

I remove the lighter from inside my shirt, light it up, and throw it in as well before taking a few steps back.

Fuck, that felt good.

COLTON

"YOU LIKE THAT?" Amy asks, riding my cock.

"Yeah," I lie, fighting a yawn. I need a drink, a hit, anything to help me out. I'm fucking bored as shit.

"Hmm," she moans, throwing her head back while her hips move back and forth.

My eyes trail down over her fake tits and thin waist. I wasn't really in the mood to fuck, but when she offered it downstairs, I thought *sure, why not*?

Someone knocks on my bedroom door.

"Go away," I growl, my fingers digging into her hips, needing more. Her boobs don't even move while she grinds back and forth like it's doing something for me, not bothered by someone trying to interrupt us.

"Colt—"

"I'm busy!" I sit up, glaring over her shoulder at the door. *Persistent motherfucker.* "Leave me the fuck—"

The door opens, and Finn leans against the doorframe. His green eyes drop to Amy's bare ass. Tilting his head to the side, he licks his lips and announces, "Raylee's here."

I smile at his words, and Amy reaches up, running her hands through my hair. "She's seen the video." I knew it wouldn't take long for her to return from her date.

He laughs, nodding once and still eyeing Amy, who has stopped fucking me. "Oh, she saw it all right. She's setting your car on fire as we speak."

"What?" I bark. Shoving Amy away, she falls off the side of the bed to the floor with a thud. "Fuck!"

"I'm sure you deserved it." Amy laughs, not the least bit upset that I just tossed her aside. We've been drinking for hours, but I'm not drunk like her, so I don't find this funny.

Not even bothering with a shirt, I run down the stairs, trying to pull my jeans up, and storm out the open front doors to see a fire raging inside of my car. "Motherfucker!"

"Damn." Alex chuckles, already on the porch, enjoying the

show. Not even bothering to stop her. "The bitch actually did it. I thought they were joking."

My teeth grind. I don't even give two shits about the car. No, I care that the pretty little princess is standing next to it, arms crossed over her chest, staring up at me with a smile on her face.

She's such a little bitch.

"Get everyone off the property," Finn orders, coming to join us on the porch. He was much slower than me coming to see the show. "We don't need an audience watching us take care of her."

"No," I disagree, not taking my eyes off her.

She's got her head cocked to the side, her long bleach-blond hair over one shoulder. She usually curls it, but it's straight tonight. I imagine walking over to her, wrapping it around my fist, and dragging her into the house and up to my room, where I tie her facedown to my bed and beat her ass with my belt. Tears running down her face while she begs me to stop before I fuck the bitch out of her. Then leave her there, face covered in my cum, unsatisfied and humiliated. That would teach her a lesson. But I also know she'd enjoy that.

"No?" Finn chuckles. "Seriously, man? She just set your car on fire." He points at it as if I don't see the flames engulfing it.

Choosing not to explain myself, I ignore him, and my eyes drop to her red heels and run up over her tan, toned legs. She wears a pair of black jean shorts frayed on the bottom with a black V-neck T-shirt. Simple yet so fucking attractive at the same time. Raylee is the devil in a woman's body. She's vindictive, manipulative, and incredibly fucking sexy. It's a sin really to look that good. And I should be ashamed of how obsessed I've become with her.

"The girl is fucking crazy," Jenks mumbles, walking out of the house with a cigarette between his lips while he lights it. His jeans are also undone, but at least he has a shirt on.

"Where the hell were you?" Finn asks him as if he would have been able to stop her.

"Getting my dick sucked." He takes a drag from the cigarette and blows it out. "Where were you?" he counters, and Finn just lets out a huff without responding.

"What did you expect?" Alex sighs, turning his attention to me. "You released that video. We knew she'd come after you."

I stand, anchored to the porch. If I make one move, I'll fucking kill her, and there are too many witnesses. Even I wouldn't be able to buy my way out of a murder charge with all these motherfuckers recording right now. No, I'll get my revenge later. When we're alone. On my time. My way.

She slowly makes her way across the driveway. One hooker heel in front of the other, head held high, shoulders back, pushing her large chest out, and her hands on her narrow hips. While she walks up the stairs, my eyes stay on hers, smoke billowing around her from people throwing water on the fire. The lights from the house make her crystal blue eyes shine, and I hate that my cock is hard, and it has nothing to do with the naked woman on the floor in my bedroom.

"Boys." She greets my friends, coming to a stop in front of me but doesn't look at them standing next to me. Instead, her eyes stay on mine before dropping to my exposed chest. "I hope I didn't interrupt you." Her red-painted lips pull down slightly for a brief second as if the thought of pulling me from a woman would make her sad. But when her eyes lift to meet mine again, a devious smile spreads across her face, telling me how she really feels about what I was in the middle of. "Shouldn't have shared that video."

I lean forward, and she doesn't retreat. No, that's one thing about this bitch. She's not afraid of anything. I get close enough to smell the smoke lingering on her clothes from what's left of my car, and whisper, "That video is nothing compared to what I'm going to do to you."

Pulling back, she cocks her head, placing her hands on my bare chest, and I tense from the contact. The softness of her touch makes my heart race. I wanted a reaction out of her but never thought she'd go this route. "I'm not worried." Giving me a fuck you smile with her signature red lips, she bats her pretty eyes at me. Reaching up, she removes a joint from inside her shirt and looks at Jenks. "Do you mind?"

The motherfucker reaches out, offering her his lighter, lighting up the joint. She takes a long drag and then blows the smoke into my face before shouldering past me into the house.

"Was that from your hidden stash?" Finn asks, watching her enter the house. His eyes are glued to her ass in her frayed shorts. He's wanted her again ever since I let them have her on the formal dining room table six weeks ago. "Dude, we should set the entire house on fire. If she's gotten into your stash, that means she's been in your room. No telling what she's planted in there."

I can't speak. My jaw is clenched shut. My hands fist, nails digging into my palms. I expected retaliation. But this? This is more than she bargained for. She has to know that I'll get her back. I'm prepared to go to war with her. And I don't lose. No matter what I have to do.

But she doesn't know why I chose to release that video now. For six weeks, I've held on to it. Patiently waiting. It was for a good reason. I'm going to make her mine. She'll spend the rest of her life being my slut.

Raylee has no idea who I really am. She thinks she knows me, but all she knows is what she cares to see. I'm just a fuck to her. She'd be terrified of us and never come back to this house if she knew who we really were.

"Put out the fire," Alex orders just as someone runs by with a bucket of water. Like that'll do anything for it. "What do you want to do?" he asks, turning to face the house, standing next to me.

"Take care of her," I growl.

He frowns, his blue eyes meeting mine. "Tonight?"

I shake my head. Tomorrow, we're supposed to have lunch with her mom and my dad, which means my revenge would only be limited to tonight. "No. I'll need more time with her."

"All we need is one night," Finn jokes. "I say we tie her up and make her our little slut like last time. Remind her how much she liked being fucked in that video."

My teeth clench. *Absolutely not.*

A white Lexus LFA Nürburgring pulls into the driveway, and I immediately know who it is. The driver's side door opens, and the guy gets out. He takes his time walking toward us. His slicked-back brown hair, penny loafers, slacks, and button-up make him look like a man who doesn't belong here. "Hey, Colton." He nods to me. "Boys." When he reaches the porch, he looks back over his shoulder.

"Nate," I acknowledge him. I've known him for years. We graduated from Barrington University with him, but we were never friends. We certainly aren't now.

He whistles, turning to face the show. "What the fuck happened?"

"Your—"

"You know how our parties get." I interrupt Finn before he can tell Nate the truth.

"Yeah, but …" Nate laughs. "Even this is crazy for you, Colt."

20

He slaps me on the shoulder before turning to face me. "Have you seen Raylee?"

Alex snorts and mumbles, "He's wishing he hadn't."

"How's that going, by the way?" Finn asks him. "You guys have been together for a while now."

Five weeks to be exact. I hate myself for even knowing that.

As if that's an odd question, Nate frowns, wondering why the fuck my friend would care about his love life. "Good." He finally answers, but his tone sounds unsure as if we know something that he doesn't.

Ahh, Raylee, your boyfriend just told on you. I bite my lip to keep from smiling. "She's up in her room," I say, pointing toward the open front doors, letting him go before anything else can be said.

"Fuck, Colt." A guy by the name of David runs up the stairs, his cell in one hand and a beer in the other. "You sure know how to piss off Raylee." He shakes his head and adds, "You guys are brave to let her live here." He laughs while entering the house.

Nate looks at me. "Ray did this?"

"Makes you wonder what Colt did to get her to go this far," Finn adds, and I narrow my eyes at him, silently telling him to shut the fuck up.

"What happened?" Nate asks me.

I shrug. "Hell if I know?" If he doesn't already know, I'm not going to ruin the surprise now. Not without her here too. That would be selfish of me.

Without saying another word, Nate walks past us into the house, no doubt to go find out what the hell I've done for her to set my car on fire.

"What do you think that's about?" Finn asks.

"He hasn't seen the video," I answer, smiling. Little Miss Priss doesn't want him to know that she's been my dirty little slut.

"I don't know about that," he argues. "It's been all over the internet. I've had over fifty people send it to me because they didn't know I was there."

I shrug. "It's the only explanation that makes sense right now."

"Want me to make everyone leave?" Jenks asks, throwing his cigarette down and stepping on it.

"Let them stay." I wave him off.

"Sure?"

"Yeah, we were throwing them a party after all." I end the

conversation, entering the house and making my way back up to my room. I walk in to see that Amy had managed to make her way to my bed, but she's naked and passed out. The thought crosses my mind to storm into Little Miss Priss's room, force her to her knees, and fuck that pretty face of hers, but I don't. Nate's in there, probably getting exactly what I want from her.

I'll let him have it for now. But it'll be his last time.

Two

RAYLEE

Pacing in my room, I've turned my cell off, unable to hear the notifications anymore when the sound of my door opening has me spinning around. I'm half expecting Colt to rush in and throw me down the stairs or drag me outside by my hair while his friends record me as I watch his car burn. But to my surprise, it's not him.

"Hey?" Nate frowns. Entering my room, he slams the door behind him.

I place my hands on my hips. "What are you doing here?" I just dropped him off at his place after our date was over.

"What's going on out there?" He points at the now closed door. "Colton's car is burning to the ground."

I wave him off. "Colt does stupid shit." Which isn't a lie. The video of me floating around on the internet proves that.

"Are you okay?" He walks over to me.

"Of course." I toss my phone onto my desk now that it won't be going off anymore. "Why wouldn't I be?" I test the waters.

"Because you're the one who set it on fire," he states, his light brown eyes narrowing at the accusation.

"Colt told you that?" *What a little tattletale.*

"He didn't have to." He takes a step toward me. "What did he do to you?"

"Nothing." I shrug.

"You're lying." His jaw sharpens. "What the fuck did he do, Ray? I'll go beat his fucking ass if he hurt you…"

"Calm down." I walk over to him and place my hands on his chest, but he pulls away from me.

"Calm down?" he repeats. "You set his car on fire. Do you not understand how crazy that was? Your mother is going to kill you."

I smile. "No, she won't." Colt won't tell her that it was me because then he'd have to explain why I did it in the first place. He'll make sure that no video is posted of what I did tonight. He has to keep up his good boy status with her because it's a part of his sick game with me. "You're worrying too much." I untuck his button-up; my adrenaline is pumping. My body is on fire, my pussy pulsating. I'm horny as fuck right now.

"Ray," he growls my name, swatting my hands away.

"What are you doing here?" I ask again.

He pulls away from me and pats down the pockets of his slacks, sighing. "After you dropped me off at home, I tried to call you but realized I don't have my cell. Did I leave it in your car?"

"No. You had it in your hand when you got out." *Lie.* I took it.

He runs a hand down his face. "I looked everywhere and couldn't find it. The last time I remember having it was when the movie was over. I had turned the ringer back on. I'm going to go look, just in case." Turning, he gives me his back.

I reach out and grab the back of his shirt. Spinning him around to face me, I wrap my arms around his neck. "I can think of something better you can do now that you're here."

I'm not stupid. He's going to see the video that Colt plastered all over the internet, but I'd like to postpone it for as long as I can. Not because I give a fuck about Nate, but because I don't want to give Colt the satisfaction of winning.

He pulls his face back, his light brown eyes dropping to my lips. "Are you high? You smell like weed."

Fuck. "Tatum was smoking. I tried it." I used to smoke back in high school, but he doesn't know that.

"Since when did you start smoking?"

I shrug. "It was just one hit." The thought of Nate coming here to look for his phone never crossed my mind. Otherwise, I would have chosen something else for my revenge. Or waited until another night.

"Raylee." He glares down at me. "What the fuck is going on?"

"Nothing. I swear."

26

He looks like he wants to argue, but instead, he reaches down, grips my bare thighs, and lifts me. I wrap my legs around his waist and allow him to carry me to my bed. I need a good fuck after the night I've had. And his dick is better than my vibrator.

Dropping me on the bed, he undoes my jean shorts, and I lift my ass so he can wiggle them down along with my thong. While he's undoing his slacks, I lift my shirt up and over my head and unfasten my bra. I lie back down, and he's hurrying to put a condom on his dick, which means he doesn't want me to suck it. I frown because I love doing that.

Once it's on, he's on top of me. His tongue is shoved down my throat, and I swallow the spit that comes along with his messy kiss. His hand goes between my legs, and I spread them for easier access. Gripping his dick, he pushes inside me. The thing about Nate is that he has a pretty decent-sized cock. He just doesn't know how to use it. Not for me anyway. I close my eyes, trying to think of something that will get me off.

My body needs a lot. The main thing for me is the foreplay. I like my sex rough and dirty. Tie me down and make me beg to suck you off. Spit on me, humiliate me. Hell, slap me around and call me your filthy slut. I promise, my body likes it. I've done my research, and a few cases say that kinks can be brought on by childhood trauma, but that's not the case with me.

I've told Nate what I like, and although he wasn't disgusted by it, he also didn't want to do it that way. He's not into that kind of stuff.

"Oh, god, baby." He groans in my ear when his hips start to move.

I run my nails down his back, and he hisses in a breath.

"Not so rough, Ray," he whines.

I want to roll my eyes. "Stop," I say with my hand on his chest.

"I thought you wanted to have sex." He frowns.

See, that was a perfect opportunity for him to slap me across the face and tell me to shut the fuck up. That's what Colt would have done. Nate's question alone just ruined it for me. But I can't stop now. I just need a better position. "I do. Let me roll over." I push on his chest some more to sit up. I manage to turn over underneath him and push my ass up in the air.

Order me to get on all fours and slap my pussy while you spit on it, my mind yells. But he's already worried about me and my recent pyro show. I don't want to scare him more.

I feel him push into me again, and he lays his chest on top of my back, pinning me underneath him. *Okay, that's a little better.*

"That's it, Ray." He pulls my hair off my shoulder, and just when I think he's going to wrap it around his fist, he pushes it to the side and gives my shoulder tender kisses. I refrain from sighing. Instead, I close my eyes and imagine that Colt is hovering over me, his hand wrapped around my throat, cutting off my air while he fucks my ass and calls me his pretty little slut.

The motherfucker has officially ruined any chance I could have at a good sex life.

———————

ROLLING OVER, I open my eyes to see Nate passed out in my bed. It's still dark outside. Getting up, I pull on a T-shirt and pair of cotton shorts and make my way down the hallway to the stairs, having to pass Colt's room and hearing a woman's voice.

"Colt! Yes ... Fuck, yeah—"

I twist the knob to find it unlocked and smile to myself before I shove it open. "Can you gag her? Not everyone wants to listen to your fake porn shit."

I see the irony in my statement, considering I was faking it with Nate just a few hours ago.

He's got his lights on, making it bright as fuck, giving me a clear view of Amy on top of him naked. Thankfully her back is toward me, so I don't have to see her tits. She throws her head back, laughing at what I said.

Colt is propped up against his headboard. His narrowed eyes meet mine for a brief second, then the corners of his lips turn up into a smirk. He lifts his hands, lacing his fingers behind his head, causing the muscles in his arms to flex at the motion. My eyes run over his smooth, defined chest, and I imagine pushing her to the side and showing her how it's done. Colt doesn't like to be on bottom. No, he prefers to be on top, holding you down while you beg for your life.

"Why don't you join us, princess?" he offers, and his green eyes drop to my shorts.

I snort at the thought. "No thanks." Then I slam the door shut and finish making my way downstairs, needing a drink of water. That weed that I smoked made my mouth dry. The party is obviously over, but there are still bodies passed out here and there. There's not much of a mess. If Colton Remington Knox has a party, you throw your shit away. No one leaves this house without cleaning up somewhat.

Grabbing a bottle of water out of the fridge, I make my way back up to my room, but I decide to make a detour and shower. My hair smells like smoke, and it's making me want to vomit.

Colt and I are the only two who have bedrooms on the second floor. Of course, he has the master bedroom with the en suite bathroom. He paid millions for this house after he graduated high school. Well, I guess I should say the trust fund money he got paid for it. His mother died when he was young, and he received a big lump sum of cash after graduation.

The guys moved in with him immediately. Alex and Jenks are on the first floor on the other side of the house. Finn has the third floor to himself.

My bedroom also has an en suite bathroom. But what's so nice about it is that you can also enter it from the hallway, so guests don't have to walk through my room if I don't want them to. Not like anyone would ever need to use mine. The house has like twelve fucking bathrooms.

Entering my bathroom, I get a towel out of the linen closet and hang it on the hook, then remove my shirt and shorts along with my underwear and step in to turn on the shower. I let the water heat while I go over to the double sinks to brush my teeth, trying to get rid of this god-awful lingering taste of weed.

I don't even smoke. Not anymore. It was my thing in high school. I hope the fucker noticed it was his. I had been in his room a few weeks ago while he was at work with his *daddy*, and I found it hidden in the back of his closet. I knew it'd come in handy eventually.

Rinsing my mouth out, I open the glass shower door and step inside, letting the hot water burn my skin. Closing my eyes, I stand under the sprayer and lean my head back, wetting my hair.

Thoughts of the video play in my head, and I think of drowning him in the pool in the backyard. How dare he record that. How dare he fucking share that. What was his goal? Why now? Why tonight?

I hate him for it, but my pussy tightens on its own just thinking about that night.

Six weeks ago

"Princess?"

I moan as my heavy eyes open, and I see Colt hovering over top of me. I'm exhausted. My body is still shaking with need. He didn't let me come. I was so close so many times downstairs in the formal dining room. Just when I was about to explode, Jenks pulled out, leaving me unsatisfied once again.

Orgasm denial is a bitch that I have a love-hate relationship with. "Please," *I whisper, reaching up to wrap my arms around his neck, but they won't move. Tilting my head back, I realize he's already tied my wrists to his bed. I swear I blacked out at one point. My lips part, and I whimper, pulling on them, making the bed rattle.*

"Just how I like you. Restrained to my bed and crying." *He runs his thumb over my lips, and I move my head, able to suck it into my mouth.*

"Oh, no." *He yanks it out.* "You'll have plenty to suck on later."

I groan in frustration, trying to rub my thighs together to ease the pressure between them. He's got every light in his room on and it hurts my tired eyes. We're both wet, fresh out of the shower. He helped wash me clean of our previous activities because I was too weak to do it myself.

He lowers his head to my chest and sucks on my nipple.

I arch my back. This isn't my first time to fuck my stepbrother. It's been going on for years. I went out with Tatum tonight. We both got wasted. An Uber dropped me off and I walked through the house to find him and his friends in the formal dining room. I actually can't remember what was said or how things went down for me to end up on my knees with my hands tied behind my back with his belt, but I've stopped questioning it years ago.

If Colt wants it, he gets it. If I want it, he makes sure to give it to me.

It's just the way things go.

"Colt, please. I need to come."

He releases my nipple and crawls his body down mine. Gripping my thighs, he throws them over his shoulders.

"Fuck—yes." *I lift my hips, practically in tears.*

He slaps my pussy, making me cry out. "You're so fucking greedy." *He growls before licking up my wetness.*

I could burst right now. My pussy is pulsing, I'm soaking wet, and I would do anything to get off at this point.

"I'll let you come, princess." He kisses my inner thigh, and I try to move my hips side to side to get his mouth where I want it.

He sinks his teeth into my thigh, making me yank on the restraints. Releasing my skin, he kisses the now burning spot tenderly. "And after you come all over my face, you're going to lick it clean. Do you understand?"

I nod, squirming. "Yes."

Another kiss, this time on my pelvic bone, and I growl at him like an animal about to attack. "And you're going to thank me."

Another yes. Or maybe I just think it. I don't know. I'm starting to see dots.

"Then I'm going to fuck your mouth and come all over your face. You'll thank me for that too."

"Anything." My hips buck when he pushes a finger into me.

"We're going to repeat that process, princess." He pushes a second one into me, and I can't breathe. My body is pulled tighter than a rubber band. "Until you pass out from exhaustion."

That night was the best kind of torture. He delivered on his promise. I passed out in his bed at some point and woke in mine the following morning. I didn't get out of bed that entire day. My body too weak, head too foggy. I knew I'd never reach that high again.

Keeping my eyes closed, I lower my hand between my legs and start to play with myself thinking about that night. Nate didn't get me off earlier in bed, so I have to do it myself.

A sound has my eyes springing open, and I go to scream out when I see I'm not alone, but a hand slaps over my mouth.

COLTON

"HEY, PRINCESS," I say, and her eyes narrow up at me.

Her hands hit my bare chest, and I take a step back, lowering my hand from her mouth now that the initial shock of me being in the shower with her is gone.

"What the fuck, Colt?" She shoves me and goes to exit the shower. But I grab her upper arm, keeping her inside.

"Get out!" she snaps, turning around to glare at me, her wet hair slapping her face in the process.

SHANTEL TESSIER

"No."

She lets out a huff. "Going to punish me for destroying your precious car?"

I laugh. I've had a few hours to calm down since the show she put on for everyone. The drinks and the joint that Finn gave me helped settle my anger. Now I'm just horny, and Amy wasn't doing it for me. But the moment I saw Raylee standing at my door, I knew exactly who would. I didn't even finish. Once Amy came, I was done with her. Raylee has ruined me for any other woman. They're boring. Unfulfilling. "Not right now." I answer honestly.

"Then get the hell out of here. I want to shower in peace."

Reaching up, I grip her wet hair, yanking her head back and making her hiss in a breath. "I want you." I don't hide why I'm in here with her. "And by the way you were touching yourself, I think you want me too." Highly doubt she was dreaming about her boyfriend since he's in her bed. If she wanted him, she'd wake him up.

"No!" She tries to pull away; her naked and wet body moving against mine doesn't help her case. "Your cock was just inside of Amy."

"Is that jealousy I hear, princess?"

She gives a rough laugh but doesn't answer.

The fact that I was wearing a condom doesn't matter, so I keep that to myself. "Here." Letting go of her, I reach over to the shelf and grab her body wash. Then grab her wrist and squeeze some into her hand. I place it on my hard cock and wrap her fingers around the base. "Clean me."

"I'm not—"

"Clean my cock, princess," I demand, placing my hands on either side of her head on the white tiled wall, caging her in. My face is so close to hers I can smell her minty toothpaste when her breathing picks up. I lower my face just as she lifts hers, allowing me access to her neck. I lick up her racing pulse, tasting the water that runs down her skin. "Clean her off me, and I'll fuck your cunt just how you like it."

"Colt." She whispers my name, and I remove my hands from the wall. Taking a step back, I place one around her neck, tightening my grip. She swallows, her chest rising and falling as a sound that can only be a whimper comes from her lips.

Fuck, she's gorgeous. Crystal blue eyes, long dark lashes,

32

and her lips… Goddamn. They were made to suck my dick. That thought reminds me that she's still holding it. "Like this, princess." I place my free hand over hers and start running it up and down my long and hard shaft, slowly showing her just what I mean. Her fingers don't even touch, my size too big for her hand. When I feel her take over, I let go.

"I hate you," she whispers, her hand gripping my cock painfully hard while picking up the pace.

I've made up my mind to make her mine, but that doesn't mean I no longer hate her. She makes me want to fuck her with my hands wrapped around her fragile throat, with the intent to kill her. The only reason I don't let it go that far is because I know she'll let me fuck her again.

"I know." I lean into her face, lips almost touching as the scalding hot water runs down both of our bodies from the sprayer to the right of me. "I fucking hate you too, princess."

"You recorded us," she says, softening her voice, making it seem like it broke her heart. As if she expected more from me. But this is what she does. Raylee could be a fucking actress. Her pretty eyes blink, her dark lashes touching her cheeks before looking up at me innocently when her hand abandons my dick.

"I did." I think she's about to push me away, but instead, her hand falls to my balls. She starts massaging them, her black painted nails scratch the sensitive skin, and I jump. She arches a dark eyebrow and squeezes them to the point I think she's trying to pop them, making my breath catch and rise up on my tiptoes. This is what I love about our hate relationship. We both take things too far. We don't think. We just act. And it's explosive. My car that is now nothing but a heap of metal and ashes proves that. "Raylee…" I warn when she doesn't let go, forcing my breathing to hitch.

She smiles up at me, and my heart picks up, thinking she's trying to push me to see just how far I'll go. Or she's trying to distract me so I won't want to fuck her. She should know me better by now.

I tighten my hand around her neck, squeezing on either side to take away her air. Forcing her plump lips to part, she's trying to breathe, but she doesn't fight me. No, my good girl takes it like the needy little slut she is. I lower my face to hers. "I just wanted the world to see how pretty you look when you're on your knees, princess."

Releasing my balls, she reaches up and slaps me across the face. She wasn't able to hit me as hard as I know she can because of the position I have her in. So I let go of her neck and take a step back, giving her a little space, and wipe off the soap her hand left on my cheek. I lift my hands in surrender. "I know you can do better—"

She punches me. Her fist connects with my jaw, making my head snap to the side. Rubbing my face, I wiggle my jaw, trying to relieve the throbbing sensation.

"Fuck you, Colt!" Shouldering past me, she opens the glass door to exit, but I grab the back of her neck, digging my fingers into her wet skin, and yank her back to me. Spinning us around, I shove her face-first into the tiled wall. She cries out, and my free hand comes around to slap over her mouth. "Shh, princess. Your boyfriend is in your bed. Don't want him to catch me fucking you."

She tries to fight me, pushing on the wall and trying to shake her mouth free of my hand, but all it does is make her wet hair slap my chest and face while the curve of her ass rubs against my hard dick.

I look down at my cock to see the water has washed all the soap off and grip the base of it. Stepping into her, I hold her against the wall with my hips and lower my head to her ear. "Now, you're going to take my cock like a good little slut. And you're going to be quiet, do you understand?"

She nods, breathing heavily through her nose.

"Good girl." I nibble on her ear. "Spread your legs for me."

She adjusts herself, doing as I say, and I take a step back from her so she can push her ass out a little. I'm too tall to be doing this shit in here, but she's got a man in her bed, and I've got a woman in mine. Neither is going to stop me, so this'll have to do.

I bend my knees and guide my cock into her pussy, groaning in the process as I stretch her open to accommodate my size. She lets out a whimper, and I reach my free hand up and grip her wet hair, pulling her head back and to the side, giving me access to her mouth. I slam my lips to hers, desperate for her familiar taste when my hips start to move.

She reaches her hands up and behind her head, her fingers gripping my wet hair while I devour her. Water filling our mouths, teeth hitting, and tongues fighting to take control.

"Play with yourself," I order, pulling away breathlessly.

Her hands drop from my hair, and I feel her fingers playing with her clit while I slam my cock into her. There's just something about her cunt that makes me weak in the knees. Maybe that's why I hate her so much—because I just can't get enough.

I close my lips over hers again, and her pussy clamps down on me, forcing a moan into her mouth. But she quickly pulls away, panting.

Needing a better position, I decide to switch things up. Pulling out, I yank her over to the far wall where there's a bench. I grip the back of her neck and bend her over. Her hands slap the wet bench while I gather all of her hair into one of my hands, then the free one slaps her ass.

She yelps.

"It's like you want him to hear us, princess. Is that it?" She shakes her head the best she can with my hand in her hair. "Want him to hear what a slut sounds like when she begs for cock?"

"No."

"You want him to walk in here and see me fucking you? Want me to show him how you like it?" I'd rather him not interrupt me right now, but I want to remind her of the possibility.

She's gasping for breath. "We shouldn't—"

"We already are." I slam my cock into her, making her cry out. With my hand in her hair, I yank her head back at an odd angle and lean over her back, growling into her ear. "I want my cum dripping out of that sweet cunt, princess. That way, when you wake up in the morning with Nate's head between your legs, you know he's tasting me."

Whimpering, she pushes her hips back into me, needing more. "Colt," she gasps my name.

"I want my cum mixed with yours all over his face." I'd be lying if I said I wasn't jealous of him. But I'll never admit that to her. He'll be gone soon enough. Once he sees that video, he won't stick around. No. He'll judge her like all the rest. She's my slut, my fucking bitch to use, and if I have to carve my name into her skin to prove that to any man who wants her, I will.

The sound of our bodies slapping fills the large shower, and I reach around to play with her swollen clit.

Her moans grow louder, and I don't even bother shutting her up this time. I love to hear her come, and whoever walks in will just get their very own show.

"That's it, princess." I bite into her shoulder before sucking the warm water off her skin. She slaps her hands on the wall in front of her to push against me. She's getting close.

I release her clit and stand to my full six-foot-two height. I spit down onto her ass and stick my thumb inside of it, knowing what she likes. What I've trained her to need.

Her pussy clamps down around me almost immediately, and she cries out, coming just like I wanted. I look down, watching my cum-covered cock slam in and out of her, and it has me right behind her.

Taking in a deep breath, I pull out of her and help her stand. Turning her around, I move the wet hair from her face and look into her heavy eyes, softly cupping her cheek. I lean down and kiss her, taking what little breath she has away.

My heart is pounding, my pulse racing, and I have the urge to force her under the water and watch her gasp for breath while it covers her pretty face.

I hate this woman so goddamn much. At least I thought I did. Now, I'm not so sure what I feel. I went public with us and what we do. She'll no longer be seen as my stepsister. Now everyone who watches the tape knows we fuck and that she belongs to me.

She pulls away from the kiss and opens her eyes to look up at me. I run my knuckles down the side of her cheek, and I see the regret written all over her face from what we just did. We haven't slept together since the night I recorded us six weeks ago. She's kept her distance from the guys and me. I've been too busy to chase her down, but things with her and Nate have gone on long enough. It was time to step in. It's the longest relationship I've allowed her to have.

She pulls away from me, and I let her get out of the shower. Running my hands over the glass, I clear the fog, and I watch as she runs out of her bathroom with the towel wrapped around her, not even bothering to dry off with it.

Leaning up against the wall, I close my eyes because of the sprayer and run my hands through my dark hair, shoving it off my forehead. Now I'm more determined than ever to make sure her boyfriend sees that tape of us together. It's going to happen one way or another. "I'm not even sorry, princess," I whisper, pushing away from the wall and turning off the water.

Stepping out of the shower, I see her lipstick on the counter and pick it up, chuckling. "You just thought you hated me."

Three

RAYLEE

I WAKE UP and stretch out my sore body, and I freeze when I hear movement behind me. Fuck, I forgot that Nate came over. I can feel how wet my underwear is from what Colt and I did in the shower just a few hours ago.

Deciding I can't fake being asleep forever, I slowly roll over to see Nate standing up and pulling his shirt on, buttoning it up before running his hands through his dark shaggy hair.

"Morning," I say softly, gauging his mood after what he saw last night.

Placing his hands on the bed, he leans over and kisses me on the forehead. "Good morning. Sorry but I have to run."

I let out the breath I was holding. "You're fine." *Thank God.*

"I've got to find my phone." He frowns, yanking his slacks on and then patting down his pockets like he did last night as if it's going to magically appear.

Not if I have anything to do with it.

I crawl out of bed and throw on an oversized T-shirt and a pair of jean shorts. Then I enter my bathroom through the adjoining door. Walking in, I gasp at what I see written across the full length of my mirror in red lipstick.

How'd I taste?

My pulse starts to race. "That fucker!"

"Is your car unlocked?" I hear Nate call out.

I grab the makeup remover, unscrewing the lid so quickly it falls to the floor, and I pour the bottle on the mirror and then run my hands through it, thinking that'll make it disappear. "No." I lie, my voice cracking on the single word. Of course, it's unlocked. I even left my trunk open last night.

"Where are your keys?"

I turn on the faucet and cup the water, splashing the mirror with freezing cold water. It doesn't do any good. *Goddammit!*

"It'll turn up." I avoid his previous question, grabbing a towel and just smearing the shit worse than it already was. When that doesn't work, I just leave it. Exiting the bathroom, I pull the door shut and meet him back in my room, trying to catch my breath while wiping my hands off on the inside of my T-shirt, hoping he doesn't see the red lipstick on them.

"You okay?" He frowns, his brown eyes looking me over.

"Of course." I give him a bright smile. "Let's go downstairs and grab some breakfast." I slide my arm through his, hoping he can't feel my body shaking.

I'm going to kill him! I knew Colt was up to something last night. Even he can't be that relaxed after what I did to his car. He had a plan, and I fell right into it.

"I can't stay. I've got to get back home," Nate reminds me.

Even better.

We walk into the kitchen, and the boys are all sitting at the table. Jenks is shoveling cereal into his mouth. Alex is scrolling through his cell while Finn is playing with his knife. Amy stands at the sink rinsing off a plate.

My eyes lock with Colt, and he leans back in his chair, a smirk playing on his face.

"I forgot to grab my belt." Nate pulls away from me, and I let him go, praying he doesn't decide to use my bathroom. I debate following him but stop myself because Colt may take that as me trying to avoid him.

Of course, he's the first to speak. "How's your morning?"

The fact that he's burning a hole in my shorts, I know exactly what he's asking. "It's wonderful." I grant him a smile. "The joke's on you. He didn't do it," I inform him, and his face falls.

"Who didn't do what?" Amy asks, and I choose to ignore her. We're not enemies, but we're also not friends. I do, however, respect the woman. She gets around, and I like that about her. She knows what she wants, and that's not to settle down. Guys

40

at Barrington call her a slut behind her back, but they're the first ones to pull out their dicks when she's around.

Colt sets down the fork and keeps his eyes on me when he asks his friends, "Boys, what's the first thing you do when you wake up with a woman in your bed?"

"Eat that pussy," Finn answers.

"Spread her legs and eat breakfast," Alex agrees.

"Devour that cunt," Jenks adds through a mouth full of cereal.

I look over at Amy, and her cheeks flush. Now I know that I'm the only woman in this house who hasn't gotten some since they woke up.

"He's not the one, princess," Colt adds, making my eyes narrow on him.

I don't plan on marrying the guy. He's just someone to play with right now. I've never been able to make a relationship last. I'm not sure what it is, but I always seem to push them away. And none of them have ever fought to stay.

"I'm out," Nate states, entering the kitchen once again, and by the smile on his face, I know he did not go to the bathroom.

Wrapping my arms around his neck, I pull him into me, making sure to put on a show. I'm not really one for PDA, but I can pretend for Colt. "I'll see you later."

Nate leans down and kisses me. I open my mouth for him, deepening the kiss, wanting to make out with him. Honestly, if he wanted to bend me over and fuck me on the island, I would pull my shorts down for him just to see how Colt reacts to that. Wonder if the fucker would record that too?

"Lunch?" he asks, pulling away.

"Yeah—"

"She can't," Colt interrupts me, and I glare over at him. "We have lunch with our parents today."

Shit! I forgot all about that. They came back this morning from their trip. "We can do dinner?" I offer.

He nods, smiling down at me. "Dinner it is." He gently kisses my lips and then turns to leave.

"Oh, Nate. I have something you might want." Colt stands at the table, reaches into his jeans pocket, and pulls out a cell phone.

My eyes widen, and I feel the blood drain from my face while my heart begins to pound in my chest.

"Missing this?" he asks Nate.

"Where did you find it?"

In my fucking car! I want to scream but can't rat myself out.

Colt smirks at me. Tossing it to Nate, he keeps his eyes locked on mine. "Someone brought it to me. You must have dropped it last night when you arrived."

Fucking liar!

Nate frowns, catching it midair. "Thanks, Colt."

"My pleasure." He sits down, leaning back in his chair and crossing his arms over his chest this time. "I also charged it for you."

I'm going to fucking kill him. And by the way he's smiling at me, the fucker is going to enjoy it. My blood is boiling, my body physically shaking. This was all part of his plan. He somehow knew why Nate came over last night. He also had to have known that Nate hadn't seen the video of Colt and me online.

"You didn't have to do that," Nate tells him.

It requires a code to unlock, so I'm guessing Nate isn't worried about Colt going through it. He honestly thinks that Colt was being a nice guy. But I know that Colt doesn't do anything unless it benefits him.

"It kept going off. I think there was some kind of emergency or something," Colt adds. "Seemed pretty serious, though." He tilts his head to the side, his green eyes looking sympathetic when he adds, "Hope everything is okay."

I let out a growl before stopping myself from jumping onto the table and slamming his face into it over and over again until it knocks all of his pretty teeth out of his fucking mouth. He already sports a bruise on his chin where I punched him in the shower. His eyes need to match.

"Okay, I'll look into that," Nate tells him before kissing my cheek.

I don't dare move.

"I'll call you later." He taps my ass and then turns to leave.

The moment I hear the front door shut, I take in a deep breath. "You ... son of a bitch," I manage to spit out through gritted teeth. I reach over, grabbing a cake that someone brought for the party last night, and throw it across the room, hitting him in the chest.

"Hey, I was going to eat that." Finn frowns, watching the chocolate chunks fall off Colt to the marble floor.

"What?" He cocks his head; his dark hair is standing in different directions, letting me know he hasn't fixed it yet. The thought of

Amy's hands in it this morning while his head was between her legs doesn't help my already sour mood. "Don't you want him to see how good you are at sucking dick?" he asks innocently.

Oh, this motherfucker. "He's well aware of that already," I counter.

There's a tick in his sharp jaw, and he stands, flicking the pieces of cake off his shirt as he walks toward me slowly. My eyes drop to his fisted hands, and I think he's planning on choking me out. I'm prepared to break my already sore hand on his motherfucking face. "Watch it, princess—"

"Raylee?"

I turn to see Nate standing under the white archway to the entrance of the kitchen with his cell in one hand and his eyes on mine.

"It's not what you think," I say defensively, knowing the moment he unlocked his phone, he watched it. I'm sure that everyone he knows has watched it by now. Who knows how many texts and calls he's had from friends informing him that his girlfriend is fucking her stepbrother?

"Oh … so you're not on your knees in the formal dining room with Colt's dick down your throat," he says slowly. His eyes remain on mine. "Because that's exactly what was happening in the video I just saw."

"It was—" I was about to say that was six weeks ago, before we got together, but I just cheated on the man this morning in the shower.

He gives a rough laugh, pocketing his cell. "Now it makes sense." Nodding to himself, he adds, "Why you set his car on fire."

I fist my hands, choosing not to respond to that. It wasn't a question.

"And you." He looks at Colt. "Why the fuck would you allow this to be seen?"

"For a day like this," Colt answers, smirking, not affected by the situation at all.

I hang my head, realizing exactly why Colt did what he did. If I was single, that video would still be sitting on his phone. It's because I started seeing someone. He wanted to sabotage it. *This is why we can't have nice things* comes to mind. Every relationship I've ever tried to have since my mother married his father has gone to shit. Granted, I was sixteen when they married, but none of them ever worked out. Now I wonder if it's because of Colt. Has he done something to ruin them for me? Well, it takes two, I guess.

Swallowing, I lift my eyes to meet his. "Nate—"

"You know, my friends told me that you were a whore." He interrupts me. "A cheap whore at that." His light brown eyes look me up and down, disgusted with himself. Like he lowered his standards by dating me.

"I'm sorry," I say wholeheartedly. I never meant to embarrass him.

However, he's not lying about me being a whore, but why is that a bad thing? Why can't I just like sex and that be okay? I first met him a couple of years ago. We went to college together, and it's not like he was a virgin. I know at least ten girls he fucked before me. How many were before that?

Nate throws his head back, laughing. "Sorry? You're a shitty liar, Ray. Just like you were a shitty fuck."

"Maybe you're the problem in that department," Colt tells him.

My eyes widen, looking over at him. He's now leaning casually against the kitchen island with his arms crossed over his cake-covered T-shirt.

"Excuse me?" Nate arches a brow and takes a step farther into the kitchen.

"You heard me." Colt uncrosses his arms and pushes off the island. "Sounds like to me that if you knew how to fuck a woman, she wouldn't fuck other men."

The fact that Colt is trying to stick up for me is irritating. I don't need him to defend me. "Stop—" I stand between them, but Colt grabs my arm and yanks me back, shoving me over into Finn who wraps an arm around my chest, keeping my back pinned to his front in an iron grip.

"A whore like her will fuck anything," Nate growls, pointing over at me.

"Obviously." Colt looks him up and down and then chuckles to himself. "She did fuck you."

Nate shoves Colt in the chest. "Watch it, Colt."

Colt takes a step back and lifts his hands in the air as if he's not going to fight Nate, his laughter growing. "Ask her who else she fucked last night?"

"Colt!" I snap, trying to fight Finn, but he keeps me held hostage.

44

Nate looks over at me, lips thinning, and demands, "What the fuck is he talking about, Raylee?"

I lick my lips nervously but can't make myself say the words out loud. It will just prove how big of a slut I really am. All his friends will be right. *The whore cheated on you, what did you expect?*

"What the fuck is he talking about?" he shouts, making me flinch.

"I—"

"And don't fucking lie to me!" His voice rises, bouncing off the white walls in the kitchen. "Did you fuck him last night while I was in your bed?"

I feel tears sting my eyes, and my body vibrates with my hatred toward Colt. Having to announce I'm a whore is harder than I expected. "Yes," I manage to say.

He just stands there, glaring at me. The look of disgust makes me want to apologize, but it won't do any good. And am I even really sorry? I did something, and I'm going to own up to it. What I did was wrong, but that doesn't mean he has to accept an apology.

Without saying another word, he turns and storms out of the kitchen. Finn lets go of me when one of the front doors slam shut.

"Guess you're free for dinner now?" Alex chuckles.

Silence falls over the room, and I swallow the knot that forms in my throat. Why am I the whore? Colt was literally fucking Amy just minutes before he was screwing me in the shower, so why am I the only one who is in the wrong? How do I know that Nate hasn't been sleeping with other women?

Colt turns to face me. "Prin—"

I slap him across the face, my teeth grinding at the sting on my palm from connecting with his cheek. He takes in a deep breath, his nostrils flaring, and I hate that tears start to burn my eyes. Instead of yelling or begging—for I don't know what—I exit the kitchen and head up to my room, needing to get away from them. I don't give a damn what Colt had to say.

It wouldn't matter anyway. We did what we did. Can't change it now.

COLTON

"THANKS FOR THE ride," I tell Finn before jumping out of his car. Since Raylee set mine on fire, I don't have means of transportation until I buy a new one.

I was going to make her take me to our lunch date with our parents, but I haven't seen her since she slapped me after I gave Nate back his phone and informed him that we fucked earlier this morning.

Entering the Victorian mansion, I find everyone already in the formal dining room. Raylee sits across from her mother, head down as she stirs the soup around in a bowl.

I pull out the seat next to her and plop my ass down.

"Good afternoon, Colton." Her mother smiles at me.

"How was the trip?" I ask, making small talk.

"It was wonderful." Her crystal-blue eyes look over at my dad, and he gives her his charming smile.

My father's butler comes up to my chair. "What may I get you to drink?"

"Water, please," I answer.

"I'll have a bottle of Moscato." Raylee lifts her hand to him.

"Raylee, I don't think—"

"I'm old enough to drink, Mother," she interrupts her mom, who just purses her lips and decides not to argue with her.

Tiffany is naturally pretty. She's got dark hair and blue eyes like her daughter. I know she gets Botox in her forehead, but other than that, she doesn't have fake lips or tits like the women my father dated before he met her. When he brought her home, I was surprised. She didn't drive a Bentley or wear a lot of jewelry. My father's always been into the flashy women who flaunt their money. Tiffany had none. I never saw her as a gold digger, though. I wasn't one of those kids that thought she was going to come into my family and try to take what's mine. No, everything was great until Raylee entered my life.

My feelings changed the moment I met her.

Six years ago

I'm in the kitchen making a sandwich when I hear my father's voice followed by a feminine laugh. They enter a second later.

"Hello, Colton," his fiancée greets me with a smile. She's got her hand in my father's, and I haven't seen the look of such pure joy on his face since—ever, really.

"Hey, Ms. Adams," I say.

"Colton, please call me Tiffany."

I nod. It's weird to see him with someone and know that they're getting married in two months. He's been dating women for as far back as I can remember, and none of them ever stayed long enough to acknowledge me.

"I didn't know you'd be here. I thought your father told me that you have football practice this afternoon."

I nod. "Yes, ma'am. As soon as I eat this sandwich, I'm leaving."

Just as I go to take a bite of my sandwich, a girl enters the room dressed in a pair of white skinny jeans and a simple black crop top. Her jeans sit high enough on her narrow waist that you can just see a tiny sliver of her tan stomach. She's got her bleach-blond hair down and in big curls.

Her crystal-blue eyes meet mine and her red-painted lips spread into a wide smile. As if it's possible, her eyes turn even bluer with excitement.

"Hi. You must be Colton." She walks over to me in her Chucks. "I'm Raylee." Reaching out her hand, she adds, "I've heard so much about you." She bats her dark eyelashes, and my mind goes straight to the gutter while my dick gets hard.

I imagine her on her knees, looking up at me while my cock fills her pretty mouth. Goddamn, this is her daughter? Why didn't my father warn me? Give me some kind of heads-up that she's fucking gorgeous.

How old is she? I can't remember what my father said. Just that he was in love, getting married, and she has a sixteen—she's sixteen. A year younger than me. My father works a lot and is always away. I overheard my father telling Tiffany that she could quit her job at the diner if she wanted to travel with him. Does that mean she'll go with my dad and leave Raylee here alone with me? Fuck, I hope so.

"Ah, yeah." I drop the sandwich on the counter and wipe my hand off on my jeans. I take her outstretched hand in mine and shake it.

"It's nice to finally meet you, Colt." A blush the color of her lips covers her cheeks, and she laughs nervously. "Sorry." She averts her eyes, tucking a piece of hair behind her ear. I have the urge to touch it and see if it's as soft as it looks. "Do you go by Colt? Or only Colton?"

She can call me whatever the fuck she wants. "Either is fine."

I clear my throat, trying to ignore my hard cock straining against my zipper. She pulls on her hand, reminding me I still have a hold of it, and I let go like she burned me.

"Well, we better get going," Tiffany states, making me jump. I had forgotten that we weren't alone. "Colton has to get to practice, and we have a dress fitting in thirty minutes."

Raylee spins around to face her mom, and her hair all but whips me in the face, giving me a whiff of strawberries. I almost come right then. My eyes fall to her heart-shaped ass, and I imagine yanking her jeans down, bending her over the counter, and dropping to my knees, eating her out as if she's my last meal.

"I'll walk you ladies to your car." My father exits the room with them, his hand still in Tiffany's.

Turning around, I face the white marble counter and pull out my phone from my back pocket. Typing out a message to one of my usual fucks.

Me: What are you doing later?

She responds immediately.

Her: Nothing. Why?

Me: Meet me after practice?

Her: Let me know when and where.

Great. I'm going to need to fuck something now that the bleach blonde has gotten me worked up.

"Colton?"

I jump at the sound of my father's voice and turn around to see him now back in the kitchen. "Yeah?"

He levels me with a stare and speaks, "I saw the way you looked at her. Don't you dare touch her." Then he turns and walks out of the kitchen.

I follow him down the hallway and to his study. "Why didn't you warn me?" I'm not going to pretend that didn't just happen. My father gave me the sex talk last year after he found what he thought was the first girl I had ever had in my room. It's safe to say he was late.

"What was there that needed warning?" he asks, sitting down at his desk.

My mouth falls open. "Seriously? Don't pretend she's not—"

"Don't go there, son." He shakes his head, interrupting me. "She's sixteen. I'm forty-five. Not only is that illegal, but that's also highly inappropriate. Plus, she's going to be my stepdaughter."

I go to open my mouth, and he adds, "And your stepsister." He glares up at me. "So keep your hands to yourself and your dick in your pants." With that, he dismisses me and starts working on his home computer.

I look over at Raylee sitting next to me in a white sundress, and it's crazy how far we've come since that first day in this house. I became a raging dick to her. But she wasn't as sweet as she put on that day either. No, she dished it back. And that is how my obsession with her started.

————

AN HOUR LATER, their staff is handing out our desserts when Tiffany looks over at her daughter. "Raylee, honey, you've been quiet. Everything okay?"

"Fine, Mom," she answers, not bothering to look up. I hide my smile behind the rim of my mimosa that I decided I needed after my glass of water was gone. Her phone goes off, signaling a text, and she pulls it out of her purse that hangs on the back of the chair.

I lean over to try to read it, but she locks the screen.

"Are you sure? You seem—" Her mother's cell phone starts ringing. She picks it up off the table. "I'm sorry, but I've been expecting this call." Her eyes go to my father, and he picks up his napkin, wiping his mouth. "We may be a little bit," she adds.

"Excuse us," he announces and then stands, walking out of the room with her.

I ignore that strange interaction and focus my attention on Raylee. Reaching under the table, I place my hand on her bare thigh.

She jumps, her head whipping around to glare at me. "Don't touch me," she snaps, shoving my hand from her warm skin.

Letting go of her thigh, I grip her wrist, twisting it and forcing a whimper out of her pretty lips. I pull it toward me until her face comes within inches of mine.

My eyes drop to her red lips and then meet her narrowed eyes. Closing the small space, I lean in, needing to kiss her. But she tosses what's left of my mimosa in my face.

I sit back in my seat, letting go of her, and she gets to her feet, grabbing her wineglass and storming out of the formal dining room.

I chuckle, running my hand down my now wet face. I catch sight of the wine bottle in the middle of the table and pick it up. Standing, I head upstairs, knowing she's running off to her old room.

So predictable, princess. She's got the door shut, but I shove it open, making it bounce off the interior wall before it slams itself shut.

"Get the fuck out!" she shouts at me.

I advance on her while she walks backward before she hits the side of her bed and falls onto it, landing on her back. I crawl on top of her, pinning her down, and grip her face. "Open up," I order and then bring the wine bottle to her lips, pouring more than I meant to into her mouth, making her choke on it. It covers her face, neck, and chest that her sundress shows off.

Setting the bottle on the nightstand next to the bed, I shove her hair out of the way and lean down, running my tongue along her neck, licking up the wine she spit up. "Tastes so good." I moan, sucking on her skin.

"Colt." She says my name breathlessly, still trying to recover from the fact I almost drowned her in wine.

"Want some more, princess?" I ask, nibbling on her ear.

"Go to hell." She lifts her chin.

I smile. "Can't we move on from this? You being a bitch and pretending not to want me?"

She glares at me. "You followed me up here. Not the other way around."

"You're right." I sigh. "I'm attracted to you, Raylee. You're fucking crazy, but every time I see you, all I can think about is fucking you."

Her eyes close, and she whimpers.

"Tell me that you don't want me," I challenge, and she doesn't respond. Smiling, I add, "See, why fight it? Just let go. We can call a truce."

"Truce, Colton?" She snorts, dragging out my full name. She very rarely calls me that. "Any chance you get, you fuck me over."

"I just want to fuck you, princess. What do you say? You and me? We can fuck the hate out of each other, whenever we want, wherever we want?"

Her heavy eyes stare up into mine. "You purposely broke up

my relationship," she argues. "You only fucked me so you could tell Nate I cheated on him."

"One, you fucked me while with another man." I give her a tsking sound and lower my lips to her ear. "Two, I was going to fuck you either way. You having a boyfriend didn't matter to me."

"You think that makes it better?" she snaps.

"I think you set my car on fire, and I ended your relationship. Let's call it even." I lick her neck, making her moan. "Now I'm offering to get you off. I'd say you're getting the better end of the deal here, princess."

"You're manipulating me." She growls.

I pull back, smiling down at her. "How so? I'm making what I want from you very clear." I shove her dress up and pull her underwear to the side, running my fingers over her pussy, noticing the way she spreads her legs a little wider for me. "You're wet." I smile, and she swallows but doesn't argue. No reason to deny what I can feel. When I shove a finger into her, she arches her neck, and her breath catches. "There's nothing wrong with being a slut, princess." I insert a second finger, and she moans. "Nate doesn't understand what that means." I remove them and push them in again while my thumb massages her clit. "If he could keep you satisfied, then you wouldn't be fucking other men."

People say all the time, once a cheater, always a cheater, but I don't believe that. Not with Raylee. Once my girl understands that she belongs to me, she'll never need or want another man. And I'll kill any guy who even tries.

I may allow others to watch me play with her, but that's only because I know it turns her on. I'll never share her again.

Reaching up, she runs her hands through her hair while arching her back. "Colt, please—"

"What, princess?" I ask, my fingers getting more forceful. Her body rocks back and forth on her bed, still pinned under mine. I add a third one, spreading her wide, and her hands grip my forearms, nails digging into my skin. "Tell me we have a truce."

She nods, sucking in a deep breath. "A truce. Just fuck me."

"That's a good little slut." I praise her, and she whimpers. "But not yet." I remove my fingers from her cunt, and she sags against the bed, her hands dropping from my arms.

I'm going to make her work for it. Standing, I grab her arm and yank her off the bed and shove her to her knees. Picking up the bottle, I take a swig and then order, "Unzip my jeans."

Her hands lower my zipper quickly, showing me just how much she wants it.

"Pull my dick out."

She reaches in and does as she's told, stroking it and licking her red-painted lips.

I tilt the bottle, covering my cock with the liquid. Thankfully, it was sitting out during lunch so it's not freezing cold. Wine drips off the sides and the head of my dick. "Drink it."

She opens her mouth and takes in my cock, sucking the wine off my long shaft. "Don't stop," I order and pour a little more on my dick; most of it covers her face and spills on her sundress. She closes her eyes, and her mascara leaves black streaks down her hollowed cheeks.

"God, you're so fucking pretty when you look like this," I say, my free hand pushing the wet strands from her face while I pour more onto my cock. Her eyes are still closed, her face is soaked and so are my jeans. But she doesn't stop sucking.

No, she takes me to the back of her throat, and my fingers dig into her hair at the scalp, grabbing her. "Fuck, princess."

She whimpers on her knees, and I take a drink of the wine while listening to the sound of my cock fucking her mouth. She sucks it like she's an alcoholic, willing to do whatever to get that last sip.

I pull her mouth from my cock, and she sucks in a breath.

"Look at me," I order.

Her heavy eyes flutter open and her lashes are wet and clumped together, lipstick smeared, and makeup completely ruined. "Gorgeous," I praise her.

Those pretty crystal-blue eyes go to the bottle in my other hand, and she licks her wet lips. "Do you want more?"

She nods, shifting on her knees. "Please."

I lift the bottle, pouring some into my mouth and hold it instead of swallowing. Lowering my head to look down at her, I spit it out all over her face. Closing her eyes, she flinches. "Lick it off," I order, and her tongue comes out, running across her lips and chin the best she can.

"Colt—"

Jerking her up by her hair, I make her cry out. I grip her chin, slamming my lips to hers, shoving my tongue into her mouth, tasting the wine. I've never wanted to get drunk more than I do at this very second. I want to drown us both in it.

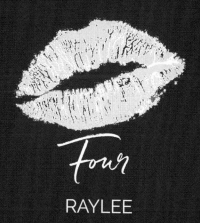

Four

RAYLEE

I DON'T EVEN try to think about how I got myself in this position twice in less than twelve hours. Or the fact that I should want to knock his head off, not let him fuck me.

Colt knows what my body wants, and I refuse to withhold pleasure from myself. If this is the only time we're not killing one another, then so be it.

He pulls his lips away from mine, and I suck in a breath. My eyes burn, I've got wine up my nose, in my hair, and my dress is soaked. I've taken a wine bath.

My body is physically shaking, and my pussy is throbbing. "Colt."

"I know." He pulls his shirt up and over his head before tossing it to the side. I reach up and run my nails down his bare chest. The defined muscles tense at the pain it causes, and he hisses in a breath. I smile, satisfied at the red marks I just left. Then he rips his belt free from his jeans and orders, "Lie on the bed."

I quickly remove my dress, underwear, and bra, and then scoot onto the side of the bed, lying across it. Bringing my heels up on the edge, I spread my legs for him. He slaps my inner thigh, making me cry out, and I slam my shaking legs shut.

He grips my hands and brings them around my legs, securing my wrists with his belt, keeping them restrained behind my knees. My arms are pulled tight, and I rock back and forth to try to loosen the tension, but it's no use.

Then I feel him step away. I lift my head off the bed to try to see what he's up to, but my legs restrict my vision. "Colt." I start to panic. Surely, he wouldn't leave me here like this, would he? Of course, he would; he's done worse. My head falls back onto the bed, my neck getting sore from holding itself up. "Colt?" I shout when I don't get a response, then jump when I feel something cool pour over my pussy, and I know it's from the wine bottle. Fuck, the UTI this is going to give me be damned.

His hands grip my hips, and he yanks me to the edge of the bed. My ass hangs off it so far that I feel like I'm going to fall to the floor.

"Try to be quiet, princess." He gently kisses my pussy, and I pull against his belt that has me tied in a knot. "I'm going to fuck you until you can't see straight. And then I'm going to come all over your pretty face."

I lick my lips just thinking about it.

His fingers dig into either side of my pussy, and he spreads my lips as wide as they will go. I bite my bottom lip to keep from crying out at the pain. Then I feel his warm tongue push inside me, and I close my eyes, a mumbled moan escaping my lips.

Letting go, he squeezes an arm between my restrained arms and legs and pulls me closer to his face. Half of my back now hangs off the side of the bed, and I can feel it slipping. Or maybe that's the alcohol. I almost finished that entire bottle of wine myself at lunch.

He licks up my pussy before sucking on my throbbing clit, and I start shaking. My eyes roll back into my head. It takes a lot to get me off, and Colt knows this. He's the only guy I've consistently fucked who can make me orgasm. He knows my body better than I do, and I hate that about him.

"Fuck, princess," he growls before shoving two fingers into me this time, and I can't help but let the cry out.

I feel like I'm falling, then realize that I have. My back is on the floor, the breath knocked out of me, and he's kneeling, shoving my legs away, forcing me to lie on my side since my wrists are restrained underneath them. He widens his legs and takes his dick into his hand before shoving it into me without any warning.

His free hand comes up, grabbing a handful of my hair, and I whimper when he pulls it back. It's hard to breathe at this angle. My arms are being yanked forward because my wrists are restrained under my knees, which happen to be in my chest, and I'm on my side. Almost like I was that night with the guys on the kitchen table.

He shoves two fingers into my mouth, gagging me while he fucks my wine-covered pussy on the floor of my bedroom at our parents' house.

He pulls his fingers out and drool drips down my face as he drops his hand to my breasts, and he pinches my nipple. I try to fight him, to pull away, but I can't. He's got me locked in place. "Colt—"

He shoves his fingers back into my mouth, his free hand still holding my head back by my hair. My eyes are watering, and I can hear his grunts while his cock slams into my pussy.

"Does my dirty slut want a dick in her mouth while I fuck her tight cunt?" he growls.

His fingers run up and down my tongue, making drool drip out the corner of my mouth and onto the floor where I lie.

"Would you like that, princess?" he asks, pulling his cock free from my pussy and then slowly pushing it back in. Teasingly, inch by inch, knowing I want it rough. "Your pussy is telling me you would. It's getting wetter just thinking about it."

I whimper, trying to suck in a breath through my nose.

"Open wide," he orders, and adds a third finger into my mouth, forcing it to stretch farther than I thought possible, and tears fall from my eyes down the side of my face. "You looked so pretty that night you had three cocks using you."

I moan, followed by the sound of me trying to slurp up the drool on his fingers when he pulls them out. I manage to suck in one deep breath before he slaps his hand over my mouth and begins to pound into me.

"But that'll never happen again," he tells me, gripping my cheeks and pulling the side of my face up off the carpet, forcing me to look up at him. "No other cock will ever fuck you again but mine. Do you understand?" To further his point, he pulls back and pushes into me painfully slow this time.

My heart pounds harder at his words. This is a whole new level that we've never played before. Colt doesn't lie, but he is a very good manipulator. He knows how to get me in vulnerable situations that require his help to get me out of.

Removing his hand from my mouth, I manage to suck in a breath while shaking my head.

Again, he moves his hips slowly, making me want to claw his eyes out. He has more patience than anyone I know. "Yes. You belong to me and only me now."

"No—"

"Open your mouth and leave it open." He shoves his hips forward at his command this time and pauses, forcing a whimper out of me. I do as he says, knowing he won't move again until I obey.

Leaning down, he lets spit drip from his lips into my mouth. I stick my tongue out for him, showing him what I know he wants to see, and he runs his knuckles down my wet cheek. "Beautiful."

My pussy tightens on his hard cock that still rests inside me. Gripping my chin, he drops his lips to mine and kisses me while his hips start to move again.

I close my heavy eyes in what I can only know as relief. I need to come. My body craves it. Demands it. And Colt knows that. No matter how big of an ass he can be, he knows how to please me.

I can't tell if I've lost my vision or if my eyes are still closed, but all I see is blackness as a rush of heat comes over me. My entire body tightens, my hands fist, and what feels like a burst of energy leaves me sagging on the floor.

He removes his lips from mine and leaves me gasping for air. My body is shaking, sweat covers every inch of my skin, and my eyes are too heavy to open.

"I'm not done." I hear him say, but it's as if I'm in a tunnel. The sound echoes in my head, and I whimper.

His hand tightens in my hair, and he yanks me to my other side, flopping me over like a fish, and holds my head in place against the floor. "Open wide, princess."

I lick my lips and do as I'm told. He pushes his cock into my mouth, and I taste myself on him. He shoves it down the back of my throat, causing me to gag.

"I'm a little disappointed. I know you can handle more."

Colton Knox has a very big dick. It's the largest I've ever had. I have a love-hate relationship with it as much as I do him. My jaw already hurts from his hand, and now it's full of his dick. Saliva pools in my mouth and runs out the side as he fucks my mouth like he did my pussy.

The sound of me slurping on his dick fills the room, but I don't even care enough to be embarrassed. At this point, there's nothing that he hasn't already done to me since our first time together.

"That's it." He yanks on my head; the side of my face is going to have a rug burn by the time he's done with me. "Open that smart mouth up for me."

I stick my tongue out, and he slides down the back of my throat. His balls hit the side of my face with the angle he has me in. I keep my eyes closed and try to suck in a breath any chance he gives me.

Then he pulls out, and I'm gasping for air as tears spill down my cheeks.

"Let's try something different." He sits me up by my hair, and I hiss in a breath. He moves me to where my back is up against the side of the bed.

He crouches down, eye level with me. My lips are parted, drool running down my chin, and my body is still shaking.

"So beautiful." He reaches up and pushes wet strands of hair from my face, and I whimper. "Shh, it's okay, princess."

"Co ... lt." I can barely get his name out. My body is wound so tight I feel like I need another release.

"Beg for my cock, princess," he softly orders, his knuckles running down my wet cheek and over my jawline. "Beg for me to fuck this pretty face, and I'll give you what you want."

My shoulders shake. I know, after last night, we've crossed a line that we can't undo. It was never like this. Not this far. We fucked but kept our distance. I changed the dynamic of our relationship—whatever you want to call it—and now, he's making me his. I went too far when I burned his car. Now he has to make a point. To me. To everyone who saw it. His previous words about only ever fucking his cock prove it.

He's claiming me. And a part of me is going to beg for it.

I swallow and lock eyes with him. "Please, Colt—"

He slaps me across the face, not too hard, but it catches me off guard, and my already soaked pussy tightens.

"Try again," he commands.

"Please?" I cry, finding myself leaning forward when he pulls away. "Please fuck my mouth, Colt. I—"

He raises his hand, and I stop begging, the motion making me flinch. I hear his laughter follow, and my face heats with embarrassment. "It's okay." He stands with his hard cock right in front of my face. He grips the base of it and slaps my cheek gently with it. "Only bad little sluts get slapped. Are you a bad slut, princess?" he asks.

"No." I manage to whimper out.

The thought of what Nate called me enters my mind, and I push it away. I am a whore. Just like he said. But Colt is offering me an out. Either I can fuck ten guys and possibly never be satisfied or I can fuck just one and get everything I need.

"No, what?" he demands.

I look up at him through watery lashes. "I'm your good little slut. Fuck me, please. I want to taste you."

He smiles down at me, nothing but triumph on his face. This is what he wants. Me, on my knees, begging for him. If it gives me what I want, then so be it.

I open my lips, expecting him to slide it in, but he doesn't. Instead, he runs it along my lips. I feel his precum, and my tongue darts out to taste it.

He moans. "Such a greedy little slut, princess." His hand goes to my hair, and he grips hold of it, forcing me to look up at him. He's wearing thin on patience.

Good.

He widens his stance, a leg on either side of me, and leans forward, his hand pushing the back of my head into the side of the mattress. I'm going to have nowhere to go. He's going to hold me captive while he fucks my face, and my mind is screaming *fuck yes.*

I've always preferred to suck dick rather than a man go down on me. A man with a head between your legs makes you vulnerable. But his dick in your mouth? That gives you control. Even if he thinks you have none. I assure you, that's not the case.

I love pleasing a man. And nothing is more satisfying than watching the guy you hate turn to a puddle in front of you because of what you're doing to him.

"Fuck me," I say, opening my mouth wide.

He groans, pushing his cock inside. Both of his hands are in my hair, and he's standing in front of me, pinning my head to the side of the bed. He's got me locked in place. All I can do is open my mouth and let him have his way with it.

He starts off with slow and deep thrusts. I look up at him, and he's staring down at me. A look of hatred mixed with pleasure in his green eyes, and I swallow while he's down my throat, forcing it to tighten around his dick.

"Goddamn." His hands tighten in my hair, making me cry out from my stinging scalp just as he pulls out. Giving me no time to recover, he shoves it down my throat again.

My entire body aches, and my abs are sore. He picks up his pace, his thrusting becoming more and more forceful while his drool-and-cum-covered balls slap my chin.

I try to fight him, gasping for a breath, but I'm unsuccessful. My hands are still tied behind my bent knees shoved into my chest. I feel dizzy, light-headed. Spots dot my vision, and just when I think I'm about to pass out, he pulls out of my mouth. A trail of drool falls from my mouth to my chest and knees, and I close my eyes, knowing what's coming.

His warm cum hits my face, and I try to pull away, but he still holds my head in place by my hair.

COLTON

I TAKE A second to catch my breath, standing in front of her while she sits on the floor doing the same. Her eyes are tightly shut, and my cum covers her face. Some drips down her chin onto her knees shoved into her chest.

Taking a step back, I bend down, pick up her shaking body, and place her gently on the bed. Rolling her onto her stomach, I lift her hips until her ass and pussy are up in the air. "I promised to give you what you want." I run my fingers over her wet cunt and up to her puckered ass, smearing her cum. "Good sluts get rewarded."

She wiggles back and forth for me, a silent beg not to make her wait. I wish I had all day, but we don't. Eventually, our parents' phone call will end, and they'll wonder where we went.

Reaching over to the nightstand, I pick up the empty wine bottle. I place the neck against her pussy and spin it around, letting it wet the glass.

She gasps and pulls away. I slap her ass, forcing her to cry out. "You'll come however I allow it. Do you understand?"

"Yes," she whines. Her ass lifts higher while she tries to adjust her wrists tied between her legs.

"Then stay still," I order and place the bottle back on her wet lips and repeat the process, getting it ready.

Once I'm satisfied, I spread her lips open wide and press the tip against the opening. She shoves her face into the bed to muffle her moan when it enters her. I hold it there, letting her get used to the feel of the cool glass.

Then I twist it, pulling it out. Her body shakes uncontrollably, and I press it back into her, giving her about an inch this time.

I smile when she pushes herself back onto it a little more.

"That's my good girl," I praise, running my free hand over the red spot on her ass cheek from her spanking. "Fuck it, princess. Back and forth—ride the bottle as if it's my cock."

She's crying. I can hear her sniffles even though she has her head shoved into the mattress, and I wish I could yank her head up, but I can't while standing behind her holding the bottle. I don't want her to hurt herself.

So I let her wallow in her own self-loathing at the fact she'll do whatever I say in order to get off.

I run my knuckles over her ass cheek, picking up some cum from before, and smear it over her ass, getting enough to push my finger into it.

Her rocking picks up, and I watch her come alive again. It's like her body is a fire—always burning. But when I touch her, it roars to life, burning bright and all-consuming. And I've decided that I'll do whatever it takes to make sure no one else gets to fan her flames.

She's all mine. Even if I have to keep her chained to my bed, satisfied and too exhausted to walk away. I don't have to love her to want her. No. Love is simple. People fall in and out of it every day. It's like the wind, changing its direction at any given second.

This is different. This is control. It's taking what I want and making her love it.

Her cries grow louder, and I watch the bottle go in and out of her pretty cunt, and I can't keep it still anymore. I start moving it with her back and forth, harder and faster. The glass is soaked, and it's dripping off her pussy to land on her legs.

I slip a second finger into her ass. "I wish you could see yourself fucking this wine bottle," I tell her, knowing she likes being treated like the cheap whore that Nate accused her of being. The only difference is he didn't do it right. I saw the way she flinched at his words. I didn't stop him because I wanted him to hurt her. It was an opportunity for her to see who he really is and that he'll never be me.

I can hear her sobbing into the bed. Her body is covered in

not only wine but sweat, and I want to lick it off. I swear there's nothing this woman could do that would make me think twice or turn me off. My hard cock is standing at attention, begging me to replace the bottle with it.

"Hmm, princess? How fucking desperate you look." I remove my fingers from her ass and spit on it, watching it run down to her pussy.

She's got the entire neck inside her, and I push it a little farther, forcing the shoulder in.

Her body stiffens in place, and she cries out, coming all over it. "That's it," I say, slowly pulling it out and holding it up to my face while she falls onto her side.

I stick my tongue out to lick it but stop myself. This isn't for me. I'm a lot of things, but I'm not a selfish lover.

Lying on my left side, I prop myself up on my forearm, facing her. I push the wet hair from her face. She's smeared all my cum on the bed along with what was left of her makeup, but it's still wet from tears. "Look what you did," I say, holding the bottle in front of her. "You made another mess."

She manages to calm her cries, looking at me. "Colt, please." Sniffing, she adds, "I need to stretch my legs." Her eyes are red and puffy, nose running.

I wish I had recorded that. I'll make her do it again another time and record it so we can watch it together while she's tied up sitting beside me. She'll beg me to touch her, and I won't until I'm ready.

I run my thumb through the fresh tears running down her face. "Lick this clean, and I'll untie you."

She nods once and sticks out her tongue. I hold the bottle in place and make her shift around, smiling while she struggles to get the right angles as her tongue curls around the neck of the bottle, licking it clean.

"That's it," I say, pushing hair back from her face, and her eyes find mine while her lips close over the top, and she sucks it into her mouth. I groan, my hard cock reminding me that I could use her mouth again. Or her ass. It's been a while since I made her beg me to fuck that.

Instead, I pull the bottle from her mouth with a pop, grab her face, and slam my lips to hers. She opens up for me and lets me taste her.

I deepen the kiss, shifting position and forcing her onto her back. Head tilted to the side for me to devour it. Pulling away, I don't say anything. I just get up, untie her, get dressed, and grab the wine bottle, leaving her lying there.

Making my way downstairs, I enter the formal dining room and see our parents haven't returned yet. I frown at that. I'm curious as to what the fuck that phone call was about. And I wanted them to catch us. I'm ready for the world to know that Little Miss Raylee Adams belongs to me. Just because I know it'll piss her off.

Five

COLTON

I'M SITTING AT the table when Raylee enters the formal dining room and plops down beside me in her seat. Her mother and my father returned several minutes ago asking where she was, and I said she had excused herself and went upstairs. They both seemed to have bought it.

Her mother frowns, looking over Raylee to find she's washed her face that is now clear of everything I did to her upstairs. Her bleach-blond hair has been put up in a wet, messy bun.

I did that!

I fucked not only her pretty face, but her tight cunt as well, and she had to shower afterward. My eyes drop to her hands that rest in her lap and see the marks left from my belt wrapped around her wrists. It makes me smile.

"Honey—"

Pushing her chair back, she stands, grabbing her purse, and interrupts her mother. "I need to go home and get some rest. I'm not feeling well," she lies.

"I'll have Janet box up your dessert to take home," Tiffany offers.

"I don't want it." Walking around the table, she gives her mother a hug.

"I better get going too." I abandon my plate and get to my feet. I already had my dessert upstairs.

"No," Raylee snaps at me, making her mother frown. "I mean, don't leave because of me. You can stay." She tries to cover herself, but the way her eyes are burning into mine confirms she's only leaving because of me.

Ahh, did the pretty princess not like how she felt when I treated her like a dirty slut? Her body craved it. Her pussy was soaked, and her mouth was willing. She needs to get used to it. Things have officially changed between us. She's letting Nate get inside her head. And I won't allow that.

"I need a ride," I remind her with an arch of a brow. "My car's in the shop."

Her jaw sharpens, and she looks away from me. I can see her body shaking. I'm not sure if it's from anger or from the orgasms that I gave her. I'm sure she hates herself just as much as she hates me. It turns me on so much. I'm still hard.

Fuck, I want to throw her on this table and rip her clothes off.

"Plus, you had that entire bottle of wine. What kind of stepbrother would I be if I made you drive after that?"

Her eyes fall on the wine bottle that sits in the middle of the table. I brought it back down here for her to see how good of a job she did at cleaning it. Not a single drop of cum on it.

I watch her cheeks go red, and she drops her eyes to the floor.

"That's so nice of you, Colton." Her mother smiles at me. "Thanks for looking out for my girl. I worry about her."

"Of course." I bite back a smile.

"That's Colt for you," my father adds. "Always the gentleman."

My little slut snorts at that, and her mother leans in, kissing her forehead. "Honey, you're sweating. Are you okay?" She places her hand on her forehead, but Raylee pulls away. "You feel warm too. You should go home and go to bed. Get some rest."

"Yes, Raylee. I think you should stay in bed the rest of the day. You must be exhausted." She glares at me. "If you're better later tonight, you can have another bottle of wine. Maybe champagne this time. They're bigger than wine bottles, ya know? Might take you less time to achieve your goal with one of those."

"I'm out." She practically runs out of the formal dining room, understanding exactly what I was saying.

"Thanks for lunch," I tell them and then follow her out the door to her car sitting in the driveway. I snatch the keys from her hand and jump into the driver's side before she can protest.

She stays silent on the way back to our house and is out of

the car the moment I come to a stop. I debate running after her but decide to let it go. The longer I let her fester, the angrier she'll be with me.

Entering the house much slower than her, I make my way to Finn's room on the third floor. I find him sitting on his bed while scrolling through his cell. "Take the video down," I tell him.

He looks up at me, pulling the sucker from between his lips with a slurp. "Sure about that?"

I nod. "It was only there for Nate to see. He saw it." After she left me alone in her bathroom earlier this morning, I got dressed and went downstairs to dig through her car. I knew she had a date with him last night, and she didn't bring him back to our house for a reason. She didn't want him to ask why she was setting my car on fire. And he wouldn't have shown up unless he wanted something from her. It had to have been his phone. That's the only thing that explained why he hadn't seen the video yet. You can only guess how excited I was when I found it in her center console.

The bitch is crazy but predictable.

His fingers fly across the screen, and then a few seconds later, he drops it to his bed. "Done."

I go to exit the room, but Alex enters. "You guys want to go out tomorrow night?"

"What do you have in mind?" Finn asks him.

He shuts the door and then walks to the end of the bed. "Mike is having a party—"

"No thanks," I interrupt him. I can't stand that motherfucker. We were once friends in high school, then Raylee came along. I told you everything went to shit the moment I met her.

"Well, I just overheard Raylee talking on the house phone—"

"Why was she on the house phone?" Finn wonders.

"Something about losing her cell." He rolls his eyes, waving his hand in the air. "Anyway, she's going to be there with Tatum. Thought we'd join them."

Over my dead body will I allow her to go to his party without me there. I guess I can tolerate him for one night. Who am I to miss an opportunity to show everyone that she belongs to fucking me now? Especially the guy she lost her virginity to.

Five years ago

I pull up to my father's house when my cell rings. "Hello?" I answer when I see it's Alex.

"Hey, man. I got some gossip."

He's such a chick. "I'm sure it's something I couldn't care less about."

"It's about Raylee."

I stop walking and spot her car in the driveway next to mine. My father bought her a car for her seventeenth birthday, and when he told her she could have anything, she picked out a white BMW. I almost rolled my eyes at her selection. She always beats me home. I have football practice after school. "I'm listening."

"She fucked Mike last night at his party."

My teeth grind. I told her not to go. Did she sneak out? No. I would have heard her. Someone would have texted me that she was there. "No, she didn't—"

"She did. Well, she tried anyway. He stopped midway. Guess she started bleeding. He didn't know she was a virgin and freaked out—"

I hang up on him and run through the six-car garage and into the house. I find her in the laundry room, sorting out laundry. She's bent over at the dryer, both hands in a dirty clothes basket, tossing certain pieces of clothing into the open washer. She has a pair of white shorts on that read juicy across her ass in gold letters and a matching white crop top, showing me her flat stomach.

She doesn't acknowledge me in any way while I stand here gawking at her. I'm a senior in high school, and she's a junior. No guy at our school would dare ask her out. I have made sure of it. She and her mother have lived with us for over a year now. I have beat guys up at school. I have paid some to pretend to like her just to make her look foolish when they dump her in front of everyone. It's childish, I know. But I don't give a fuck. I've wanted her and couldn't have her. So it was just easier to make sure that no one else would either.

But a virgin? I expected her to be somewhat experienced. Not innocent.

She finishes what she was doing and turns on the dryer and then the washer. Spinning around to leave, she finds me standing in the doorway, blocking her exit to the hallway. "What do you want, Colt?" she huffs.

"You let Mike fuck you?" I bark out, unable to mask my temper.

Raylee just rolls her eyes. "Who I choose to fuck is none of your business." She goes to shove me out of the way, but I place my hand on her chest, pushing her back. "Get out of my way!" she snaps.

"Make me."

Her fists hit my chest, catching me off guard, and I stumble back, but not enough to allow her to exit. I grab her wrists and slam her back into the wall, shoving her arms above her head and pinning them in place.

She's glaring up at me, breathing heavily.

I cross her wrists to hold both in place with one hand. The other drops to her waist, and I place my hand on her warm skin, making her suck in a deep breath. "Did he make you come?" I ask.

Her body stiffens against mine at my question. Those crystal-blue eyes grow heated, and her lips part. I let go of her wrists, and her arms drop to her sides, but she makes no move to push me away. I keep my hand on her waist while the other cups her jaw. My thumb runs over her parted lips. "Tell me, princess, did you at least get off?"

"No," she breathes.

"That's good to know."

Her eyes narrow once again, and she opens her mouth to curse me when I add, "That's my job."

She swallows, and I let my eyes drop to her heaving chest. My hand slides farther up to her rib cage. I dig my fingers into them as she begins to pant. "Colt, we can't—"

"Of course, we can," I interrupt her. "Beg me, princess." Lowering my lips to her ear, I hear her intake of breath. She smells like strawberries and bananas. My cock is so fucking hard just thinking about her and me in my bed. It always is for her. But I haven't made my move until now. "Beg me to make you come."

"I … uh…" She stumbles over her words.

The thought of her being so inexperienced makes me smile. "You don't have to be shy about it. Just say what you feel." Pulling back, I run my thumb over her bottom lip. "Did he fuck your mouth?"

Her body trembles against mine as she gently shakes her head. I push my thumb between her parted lips just a little. Then I remove it, pulling on her bottom lip in the process. "I want to fuck your pretty face."

Those crystal-blue eyes always glaring at me are anything but right now. They're so big, trained on mine. I like it. She's not dropping her eyes to the floor or pulling away. No. She wants me to make her my slut. I feel like I've wasted the past year of my life with her being in this house by not using her. "What do you say?" I ask. "I fuck your mouth and then your cunt until we figure out what you need to get off?" I'm not sure what she'll like, but I'm willing to spend my entire night figuring it out.

"Okay," she whispers, licking her lips.

I pull away, grab her hand, and drag her up to my room before she changes her mind.

"We're going to Mike's," I say, pulling myself out of that memory.

In a way, it's my fault how she turned out. I fucked her every way you could think of that next week. On the hood of her car out in the middle of nowhere. In the back seat of mine while in the driveway. In her bed and mine. The shower. Hell, the next day, she sucked my dick right there in the laundry room. You name it, we did it. She was addictive. The dirtier it got, the wetter her pussy was.

Alex nods. "Then it's settled. I'll call Jenks and let him know."

RAYLEE

"HEY, MOM," I say, entering the kitchen back at her and Cliff's house.

"What?" She spins around, pushing her glasses up her nose. "Hey, sweetie. Twice in one day? That's a surprise." She drops the cookbook she was holding and walks over to me, pulling me in for a big hug. "How are you feeling?"

"Better." My arms hug her tighter. I've always been close with my mother. She was all I ever had.

Pulling away, she walks over and pulls a barstool out, and pats her hand on it. "Have a seat. I'm about to start making dinner."

"Oh, I can't stay. I realized I left my phone here earlier." Of course, Colt had distracted me, and I forgot it upstairs. Pretty sure it's still on my bathroom counter where I set it before I jumped in a quick shower after he gave me a wine and cum bath.

"Well, I'm glad you did. How are things going with Nate?" she digs. "I was hoping you'd bring him with you today. Cliff and I would like to meet him."

Thank God she didn't mention that at lunch; Colt would have jumped all over an opportunity to make a stab at me for that. "We broke up," I tell her.

"Oh." Her voice softens as if my statement just gave her a reason as to why I was acting strange today. "Well, you'll meet the right one. It just takes time."

"I know, Mom." She's a hopeless romantic at heart. My father treated her like shit. The best thing he ever did was leave us. I'm thankful he never tried to return. "I'm still in college." I'm about to go into my senior year. The last thing I need is anything serious anyway. I've seen girls give up their entire future for a fucking dick. Yeah, I want to know how that works out for them five years down the road.

"Look at Cliff. It took a long time for me to meet him. But believe me, the wait was worth it." She sighs dreamily, looking off into nothing. "Well, I can't say that." Correcting herself, she adds, "I wish I would have found him sooner for us. We're lucky to have him and Colton in our lives."

I roll my eyes and agree, hoping she doesn't hear the sarcasm. "The luckiest."

"Hey, babe—" Cliff enters the kitchen but cuts himself off when he spots me. "Raylee. This is a pleasant surprise." He smiles at me.

For an older guy, Cliff is hot. He takes care of himself, works out, and eats healthy. He's got that salt and pepper thing going on, over six foot tall with dark green eyes and a gorgeous smile. Just like his son. If I knew him in a different life, I'd totally fuck them both. At the same time. No questions asked.

"Don't get too excited, dear. She just forgot her phone." My mother laughs. "Who called you?" she asks as he places his cell in the pocket of his dress slacks.

"It was Colton." He frowns. "I had called him earlier after he left about his car, but he didn't answer. That was him calling me back."

"What did he say is wrong with it?" she wonders, my mom, always concerned.

"He said it can't be fixed."

"What?" She laughs. "That's silly. He paid a million dollars for that thing. What does he mean it can't be fixed?"

Oh, so her *good boy* lied to them about how much his car

cost? He probably doesn't want his daddy to know how much of his trust fund he spent on it.

"I don't know." He sighs. "I offered to have it towed to a guy I know and have him look at it. Something has to be able to be done. He said no. That he had it taken care of."

I snort, and they both look at me. Placing my hand on my chest, I fake cough. "Sorry, something is in my throat."

"Here." My mother opens the fridge door, which is made to look like a cabinet, and hands me a bottle of water. "Drink this. It'll help."

I don't even open it.

"Well, if he says he has it handled ..." she trails off, shrugging.

"Yeah." He walks over to her and kisses her forehead. "I'm going to be in my study. I've got some work to do before dinner."

"Okay."

"Don't be shy, Raylee." He points at me. "Your mom is going crazy being here all by herself ever since you moved in with Colton and the guys."

I bet. I've been living with him for three years now.

"Dinner will be ready in an hour," my mom calls out to him as he walks down the hall.

"Well..." I push off the barstool. "I'm going to go upstairs and get my phone, and then I'm going to leave."

"Sure you can't join us for dinner?" Sticking her bottom lip out, she pouts, and I laugh.

"Not tonight. I've got plans." *Lie.*

"Okay." Walking over to me, she gives me another tight hug and whispers, "I love you."

"Love you too, Mom." Pulling away, I make my way upstairs and to the bathroom. My phone sits on the counter next to the sink with ten new texts and three missed calls. Tatum finally called our house earlier when I wasn't answering my cell, worried about me. I still had it on silent from all the video notifications. Otherwise, I would have heard it ringing while Colt and I were up here earlier.

Three texts are from Nate. I don't even open them. I'm sure there's nothing he could possibly need to say to me that I would want to hear. I already know I'm a whore. Don't need his reminder.

Exiting the bathroom, I stop and look down the hall to Colt's old bedroom. I find myself walking over to it. Pushing the door open, I flip on the light.

74

He's such a guy. Walls covered with football posters; shelves covered with sports memorabilia. He's got pictures of him and the guys up on a poster board that Macey Johnson made him his senior year of high school. The girl was obsessed with him. They all were.

I walk over to his king-sized bed and sit on the side. It all started in this damn bedroom. My body came alive. It had been begging for what Colt made it feel.

I knew he hated me. He treated me like shit. But in here, things were different. I liked it. The hateful words he normally spewed at me sounded different when we were both naked. They felt just as cruel, but it was like he said it in a different language that only I could understand.

He wanted me.

He was hard for me.

He came for me.

Colt wasn't a virgin. And let's just say my first time wasn't what I thought it would be. But isn't it that way for most girls? Colt made my second time mind-blowing. And the third. And the fourth. Fuck, it was so good that I had aftershocks. Fucking tremors.

Lying back on the bed, I fan out my arms and close my eyes, remembering that day like it was yesterday. Not five years ago.

We crash through his bedroom door, and he pulls me to a stop. "Get undressed," he orders.

I pull the crop top up and over my head and toss it to the side. Then I shove the Juicy shorts down my legs along with my underwear. When I stand to my full height, I realize he's leaning up against his now closed door. Still dressed.

My heartbeat accelerates, and I place my hands over my chest. Panic turns my stomach. This was a prank. His friends are going to jump out and laugh at me. Maybe even take pictures of me.

He hates me. Has never been nice to me or shown any sexual interest in me. Why would he now? Stupid Raylee. I always told myself I'd never be one of those girls, yet here I am. Tears sting my eyes and I lower them to my bare feet.

Deciding to run for it, I try to get out of his room but he's blocking the door. "What's wrong, princess?" he asks in that condescending tone.

Princess isn't a term of endearment. It's a nickname he's given me to belittle me. And I hate it.

"Let me out." I sniff, head still down, now looking at his tennis shoes. My room is just down the hall, but no one is home. And the maids won't be here until tomorrow.

Placing his hand under my chin, he lifts it, forcing me to look up at him. "You're not going anywhere."

"But—"

"I'm going to fuck that pretty face, remember?" His voice is soft, almost loving. His green eyes search mine before dropping to my lips. "You're going to be a good slut for me."

I whimper, my thighs tightening. Why do those words turn me on? I can feel the wetness running down my legs. It's wrong. We're taught not to be objectified. To have self-respect. Know our worth and demand more than that. So why does my body react in a way that it shouldn't?

"Don't cry." His free hand comes up and cups my face. "Not yet anyway. I haven't even gotten started."

"Colt," I whisper his name, my body trembling. He can probably hear my heart pounding in my chest.

Leaning in, I stay rooted to my spot, and he gets close enough that he licks up my cheek, tasting my tears. My body breaks out in goose bumps, making me shiver.

"Get on your knees, princess. Show me how pretty you are when you beg." His hand grips my hair, and he yanks my head back, making me cry out. His free hand grips my neck, holding me in place, and I think my legs are about to give out. "Beg me to fuck this pretty mouth like the slut that you are."

Fresh tears sting my eyes at his words. I'm not supposed to be turned on by this. I'm not supposed to want him. But I can't explain this need to submit to him. To be his slut.

He lets go of me and takes a step back. Leaning against the door, he crosses his arms and his ankles. His green eyes stare at me expectantly, waiting for me to give him what he wants.

Taking in a deep breath, I fall to my trembling knees, naked in the middle of his bedroom, and look up at him. Swallowing the lump in my throat, I manage to get out the single word. "Please?"

He gives a rough laugh. "Oh, I've got a lot of work to do."

His words piss me off. My eyes narrow on him, and I stand on my shaky legs. Walking over to him, I lift my chin. "Know what, Colt? Fuck you!"

A wide smile spreads across his face, making his green eyes light up with pleasure. He's enjoying this. Playing with my emotions. I can't tell if he wants me to cry my eyes out or slap him across the face at this point.

It makes me question everything about him. His motives for what he said to me downstairs in the laundry room. Why he brought me up here. His interest in me is giving me whiplash.

"Move," I demand, placing my hands on my naked hips. "Now."

He shakes his head slightly, making a tsking sound. "Oh, princess, princess—"

"Quit calling me that," I shout, my hand coming up to slap him.

His head snaps to the side, and I place my hands over my mouth, gasping. Time seems to stand still. I've never hit anyone. God, how I've wanted to do that to him a million times, but I didn't dare do it.

Panic knots my stomach, and I know I have to do something. "Colt, I'm—"

He reaches out and grabs a handful of my hair, cutting off my apology, and drags me across his bedroom.

"Colt!" I scream his name, trying to fight him off. But he's too strong, and I can't reach behind me to shove him away. He bends me over the side of his bed, pressing me facedown into the mattress. He stands behind me, bending over as well, pinning me under him. "Co … lt," I whimper, my hands now digging into his comforter, trying to push myself up, but he's on top of me. "Please." I gasp, tears stinging my eyes. He's still got a hold of my hair, and he's holding on so tight it stings. "Please." I sniff as they spill over my bottom lashes and run down my face. "I'm sorry." I lick my wet lips. "I'm sorry … please …"

Letting go of my hair, he gently brushes it off the side of my face, and I begin to sob underneath him. My mind is trying to understand why my pussy is wet and begins to throb when I feel his hard dick against my lower back.

"See, princess." He slides his hand to wrap around my throat and grips my chin, holding my head in place and lowering his lips to my ear, whispering, "You're learning already."

My eyes spring open, and I sit up, looking around his bedroom. I learned a lot in this room. Our parents were out of town for three days. He spent that entire time pushing my body in ways that I didn't even know existed.

Then, when they returned, he was back to the dick he always was, in the language that everyone else understood. Like I never crawled across this floor, drool running from my mouth, begging him to fuck me in ways that made me disgusted with myself.

It got worse after that. Thankfully, he never looked at me while at school. Actually, school was my only safe place. The only friend I had there was Tatum. Colt hated that too. She's Alex's little sister. So wherever she was, I was.

Getting up, I turn off the light and shut the door, forgetting that I ever gave Colton Knox anything but satisfaction for being his slut.

———————

WALKING INTO OUR house, I listen and soak in the silence. Which is odd for a Saturday night. Maybe the guys went out to a party or something. Who knows? I don't keep tabs on Colt. He does whatever the fuck he wants with whoever he wants.

Deciding I need a drink, I go to the wine cellar that's off to the right from the garage. It's large enough to be a fucking bedroom. Why he thought he needed a house this massive is beyond me.

Pulling a bottle of wine down, I pop the cork and grab a glass from one of the cabinets. Pouring the wine into the glass, I accidentally fill it all way to the rim. Thoughts of pouring it over my naked body and sending a picture of it to Colt does cross my mind. The shock factor alone would be worth it. I've never sent him pictures of myself. Hell, we don't even text or call one another. But I guess I don't need to when he's got fucking videos of me on his phone.

My cell ringing in my pocket has me pulling it out. "Hey?" I ask when I see it's Tatum.

"You found it."

"Yep." I go to take a drink, but it's too full. So I lean over and slurp it off the top.

"What are you doing?" she asks.

"Getting my drink on. Want to join me?"

She sighs heavily, letting me know she's fighting with Billy. "The house is quiet, which can only mean the guys are somewhere else fucking shit up tonight. Come over. We can have a sleepover. Scary movie and drinks on me."

Her laughter grows. "You twisted my arm. I'll be there in ten."

"See you then." I hang up and pocket my cell. Then I turn and look over the wine bottles, trying to think how I'm going to get four bottles upstairs to my room without having to make several trips.

Six

COLTON

I SIT IN the driver's seat of a blacked-out Cadillac Escalade. Finn sits in the passenger seat, playing a game on his cell. The sound of gunfire is giving me a headache.

"Fuck yeah—Die. Die, you motherfucker…" He practically comes off his seat while screaming at it.

"You're rocking the truck, man," Alex snaps, kicking the back of Finn's seat. "How are we supposed to go unnoticed if it looks like someone's fucking in here?"

Jenks laughs from behind me.

"You're just jealous because I killed you three levels ago," Finn replies.

Alex huffs, sitting back in his seat.

My cell rings through the Bluetooth, and the sound makes me jump. Unknown caller shows up on the screen. "Turn it off." I slap Finn's shoulder, and he stops immediately, dropping it to his lap.

"Hello?" I answer.

"You in position?" our boss asks, straight to the point. The sound of thumping bass can be heard in the background at his club.

"Yes, sir," I respond, looking around the abandoned parking lot before us. We're tucked away in the very back, underneath some trees where there aren't any lights. "Should be any moment."

"Good. Get it done." He hangs up, and I sit back in my seat.

Finn picks his cell back up, going back to his game.

Our boss is a sadistic son of a bitch, but I like him. He's a no-bullshit kind of guy. We've worked with him for a little over a year now. He recruited us our senior year at Barrington University.

One year ago

It's dark out here in the middle of nowhere. The feel of the gun tucked into the back of my jeans gives me comfort, knowing that if I have to, I'll blow someone's head off.

Car lights shine on the road at the end of the gravel driveway before they turn onto it and head toward me. The white ZO6 Corvette rolls to a stop, and Finn jumps out, wearing a black leather jacket, white T-shirt, and jeans. He's got his hair slicked back and a joint tucked behind his ear. He looks like he's about to have a photo shoot for GQ or some shit.

"What the fuck are you doing?" I ask, looking him up and down.

He grabs the collar of his jacket and pops it. "It's not every day you get an invitation to the Cathedral by a Lord."

I chuckle. "He doesn't want to fuck you." Reaching out, I steal the joint from behind his ear, and he pulls a lighter out of his jeans pocket, lighting it for me. "I mean, unless he's into that kind of thing." I take a drag and close my eyes, holding it in.

He snorts. "I fuck women in the ass. I'm sure a man's is no different."

I choke on the smoke I was holding in my mouth, and he laughs, taking the joint back. "Pretty sure you'd be his bitch," I say through laughter. "Not the other way around."

Another set of lights pulls in, and a red Maserati rolls to a stop next to the Corvette. Jenks gets out of the driver's seat, and Alex crawls out of the passenger side. "You guys ready?" Alex asks, spinning his baseball hat around backward. He's dressed in a plain black T-shirt and dark jeans with tennis shoes. The fact that he's wearing a hat tells me he doesn't give a fuck about his appearance tonight. Jenks has on light jeans and a white hoodie. Also, no fucks given.

"Been waiting on you guys." Finn puts his joint out, and I roll my eyes at him. He makes it sound like he's been here for twenty minutes.

"You guys packing?" Alex asks.

"Yep," we all answer.

The Lords aren't known for their communication skills. They shoot first and never fucking ask any questions. We walk up the steps to the Cathedral, and I push the double doors open; they squeak like they haven't been used in years.

"I've heard this place is haunted," Finn whispers.

Alex snorts. "Since when do you believe in ghosts?"

"Think about it, man. This would be a paranormal lover's dream. All the people who have been killed here over the years, plus the cemetery behind it ..."

Someone clears their throat, cutting off Finn, and I turn to see none other than the man who is offering us the chance of a lifetime. He's dressed in a black button-up shirt, sleeves rolled up his forearms, with black slacks and matching shiny shoes.

There are whispers about the Lords all over Barrington University. But you don't know who actually is one. You have to be born into their secret society. Have their bloodline. But even that doesn't guarantee that you will become a member. They have to endure years of initiations. I'm talking bloodstained-hands type. I'd join in a heartbeat if they would let me.

Alex steps forward. "Mr. Crawford—"

"You guys have weapons on you?" he interrupts him, not caring about introductions. He knows who we are.

We all nod.

"Hand them over," he demands.

I pull the gun out of the back of my jeans and hand it to him. He removes the magazine and pulls back the slide, popping the bullet out that I had chambered. Then he tosses the useless gun to the ground. The sound of metal meeting concrete makes me cringe. The echo is ten times worse.

Finn pulls out his knife and hands it to him. He tosses that too. And so on with Alex and Jenks until we have nothing to protect ourselves with.

"Let's go," he orders and turns around, walking us down the aisle. I look around at the rows and rows of empty church pews. There are stairs on either side at the front of the room that lead up to a loft. In the middle sits what looks like a baptism pool, but there's no water in it right now.

"I feel like it's illegal for us to be here," Finn whispers.

"Shouldn't we sign an NDA?" Alex asks.

Tyson spins around, forcing us all to come to a stop. His dark brows turn down. "An NDA?" he repeats like it's a word he's never heard of before.

"Yeah." Alex nods. "Or prick our fingers. Sign our lives away with our blood," he jokes. "Otherwise, how else do you know we aren't going to go and run our mouths about this place and what you're going to pay us to do?"

The Lords take their oath of silence and duty very seriously from what I've been told. They will kill or die for it.

"I see." Tyson nods once, tucking his hands into the front pockets of his black dress slacks, and steps into Alex. The others and I all take a step back, giving them space. "If you so much as say one word about me or anything I have you do to anyone other than who you see in this room right now, I'll take a knife and cut both of your Achilles' tendons out." Alex swallows. "And then I'll sit back and drink a glass of whiskey—neat—while I watch you crawl across the floor on your hands and knees with snot and spit covering your face, sobbing like a little bitch, begging me to end your pathetic fucking life." Tyson gives Alex a chilling smile. "How's that for an NDA?"

"I'm good with that." Finn nods quickly, throwing his hands up. "I don't need an NDA. My lips are sealed. I like walking."

Silence then falls over us, and a coldness runs up my spine. Maybe Finn was right about this place being haunted.

Understanding that we know the bastard isn't joking about his sadistic idea of torture, Tyson seems satisfied with our silence and turns, giving us his back, walking off to the right at the front of the pews through a door.

Jenks slaps Alex in the arm and whispers, "What the fuck, man?"

Alex just shrugs.

We walk down a hallway and take a left through a new door. It's a narrow, spiral staircase down to a basement. When we get to the bottom, Tyson shoves open another door, and we step inside.

"Holy shit." Jenks gasps.

Holy shit is right. It's set up as an underground triage. It's bright as fuck with large fluorescent lights hanging from the ceiling. There are a couple of hospital beds, monitors, and instruments scattered across metal tables. I also don't miss the drains placed in the floor around the room. Makes me think they're there for easy cleanup.

"What is all this?" Alex asks.

84

"Are you left or right-handed?" Tyson asks him, ignoring his previous question.

"Left," he answers.

"Come here." Tyson walks over to a chair in the middle of the room and pulls up an armrest, locking it in place. *"You'll go first. Lay your right arm out on the armrest. Palm up."*

Finn looks at me, his green eyes wide, and I shrug. I wasn't given a fucking itinerary.

Alex plops down in the chair, laying his arm out while Tyson walks over to a table and grabs three black straps that resemble belts. Going back over to Alex, he orders, "Open your hand." *He places one of the belts right in the center of his palm.* "Make a fist," *Tyson adds, and Alex does so, wrapping his hand around the leather. Tyson pulls it tight enough around the armrest to make Alex flinch and then buckles it in place underneath. Then he does it again with the second belt in the middle of his forearm, securing his arm to it. The third he throws in Alex's lap.* "That one goes in your mouth to bite on."

"What—?"

We all turn around when the door behind us opens, cutting off Alex, and an older man walks in with a fucking doctor's coat on. "Good evening, gentlemen." *He smiles.* "Please, everyone have a seat. Get comfortable." *He gestures to the chairs and hospital beds that sit around the large space.* "We've got a long night ahead of us." *He then walks over to a table that has what I can only guess is a tattoo gun on it.*

"We're getting tats?" Jenks questions.

"No. I'm not qualified to give those. An artist, I am not." The old man laughs at his own joke.

"Then what the fuck is it?" Alex growls, trying to pull his arm free of its restraints.

"This is as close to an NDA as you're going to get," Tyson states. Walking over to a table at the back of the room, he picks up three backpacks and then comes over to drop them at our feet. *"It's your key to the castle, so to speak."* He widens his stance and crosses his arms over his chest. *"And it's going to hurt like a bitch."*

"Your clock has to be off," Jenks argues from the back seat, pointing at the dash.

"It's not wrong." Finn shakes his head, still playing that damn video game.

"We were told one o'clock."

"They'll be here," I assure Alex.

"We're going to be late. I'd rather not get my balls cut off by Ty, thank you very much," Alex snaps.

Finn laughs. "He'll make you eat them if you call him *Ty* again. I swear that dude hates you with a passion. *Do we need to sign an NDA?*" He jokes about that night at the Cathedral.

"Shut the fuck up." Alex slams his fist into the back of Finn's seat. "At least I didn't cry."

"I did *not* cry," Finn says defensively. "I'm pretty sure I blacked out, though. Fuck, I still have nightmares about it." He laughs at himself. "That shit hurt."

Goddamn right, it hurt.

Lights pull into the parking lot, and I sit up straighter. "Showtime."

I hear a backpack being unzipped in the back seat, and then a black mask is thrown into my lap, followed by a black hoodie. I slip them both on. Then I remove my gun from the driver's side door pocket and cock it, making sure the safety is off.

"Motherfucker," Finn hisses.

"What?" I ask, looking over at him, and he's leaning forward, staring out the tinted windshield, his black mask already in place, gun in hand.

"He brought his daughter," he growls.

"We'll just bring her—"

"No," I interrupt Alex.

"We can't leave her. She's a liability that I'm not going to take the fall for," he argues.

"I'll take care of it," I say, reaching my hand out. "Someone hand me a backpack."

Jenks places one in my hand, and I open it up, digging around inside to find what I need and slide it into the pocket of my hoodie. I gotta hand it to Tyson. He is always one step ahead. I swear the Lords have every drug known to man just stashed somewhere in case they need it for some fucked-up reason.

Seconds later, another car pulls up, and the man gets out. The guy we're here for points at his daughter and makes the introductions. We don't have a very clear view. They're not standing under a light, and they've got their headlights off.

"What kind of sick man brings his daughter into this shit?" Finn wonders.

"Maybe she's into it," Jenks offers. "Women can be just as fucked up as men. Don't be so sexist, Finn." He laughs jokingly.

The statement makes me think of Raylee and our afternoon in her bedroom. I haven't seen her since, but I can still taste her and the wine. Fuck, I want to pour champagne all over her and lick her clean.

"It's done. Let's go," Alex orders.

I throw the SUV into drive, keeping my lights off, and slam on the gas, tearing across the parking lot. Bringing it to a quick stop next to the Jaguar and Town Car, I barely have it in park before the guys are already jumping out.

Screams erupt as the guys grab the man, and I reach for the girl but not before she gets a fist to Finn's face.

"Motherfucker!" he growls.

"Let him go," she cries, jumping on his back like a fucking monkey, wrapping her arm around his neck, choking him.

"Get the fuck off me," he growls, letting go of the man he was holding. The man goes to run, and I lift my gun, shooting him in the head. The sound leaves a ringing in my ears. He drops like a rock, blood now running down his face.

Putting my attention back on Finn, I watch as he slams his back into the side of the Cadillac, smashing her between it and him, knocking her off. He's gasping for air and yanking at his mask but not removing it. "Fuck, she's ballsy." He grunts.

"Hold her facedown," I snap, pulling the syringe out of my pocket and biting on the end to remove the cap.

"Don't touch me!" she screams as he grabs her hair and yanks her to the ground. He then straddles her ass and grabs her hands, pinning them behind her back. I kneel and yank the collar of her shirt down, sticking her in the neck, and she's out cold instantly.

We both stand and look over the now unconscious girl. Dark red hair fans out around the concrete while she lies motionless. "Put her in the car. I'm going to see if the guys need help," I say, picking up the cap and putting it back on the syringe before placing it in my pocket.

Tucking my gun back into the waist of my jeans, I walk around to the rear of the Escalade and find the guys tying up our assignment. "Did he give you any trouble?" I ask.

"Nope." Alex pulls the zip tie tight around his wrists behind his back. "Fucker passed out immediately."

"Go ahead and shut the hatch. I'm going to sit back here with him." Jenks nods at me, jumping inside.

Once Alex moves out of the way, I push the button to close it. "Let's go," I order Finn, watching him over by the Jag.

"We'll follow you to dump the Town Car," I tell Alex, and he nods.

Getting into the Escalade, I watch as Finn closes the driver's side door to the Jag before walking over and hopping into the passenger seat, and then I drive off.

———

FORTY-FIVE MINUTES later, I'm pulling into the lot behind Blackout—the club that Tyson Crawford owns. I don't know his story, and I'd never fucking ask. But from what I've heard over the years about the Lords, he's not the typical member.

We all get out, and I walk over to the door reserved for the Lords and us.

Undoing the watch on my left wrist, I move it down around my hand to reveal the black triangle tattoo that has four lines through it. It's our NDA, as Tyson so nicely put it. The key that grants us unrestricted access to his dark and grim castle.

I slide it under the scanner, and the green light runs over it before the door unlatches. I place my watch back in place to hide it and pull on the steel handle just as Alex comes walking up with an unconscious man over his shoulder. I hold the door open for him and Finn, then Jenks. Locking the SUV, I wait to hear it beep before I pull the door shut.

This entrance takes you straight to the basement, underneath the sounds of the busy club. We make our way down, and I see Tyson standing by a man I know. Not well, but I used to see him around Barrington University.

"You're late," Tyson snaps.

"They were late," Alex growls, tossing our assignment onto a metal table. "You're welcome."

The man shakes his head, chuckling. "I see what you mean," he says to Tyson and then pushes off the wall. "Gentlemen, I'm Ryat Archer." He reaches out his right hand, and I shake it.

"Colton Knox."

He nods. "Ty just filled me in on what you guys do." Ryat finishes his introductions. "How do you like working for the Lords?" he asks.

Alex snorts. "We don't work for the Lords. We're just Tyson's bitches."

Ryat whistles, looking over at Tyson, who points at the door. "You can leave whenever you want. Just cut that brand off your wrist."

"I'll bleed out." Alex scoffs. "It'd be suicide."

Tyson just gives him a chilling smile as if that's the point. The only way out is death. "What's the damage?" Tyson asks us.

"Colt shot one, and I got one," Alex informs him. "Car and bodies disposed of."

Tyson nods to himself. "So only two dead. Not bad."

"Well, at least we didn't kill this one," Finn offers, pushing his dark hair back from his face. He's got a bruise already under his right eye from the bitch back at the pickup spot.

We were ordered to deliver one client, unconscious but alive. Anyone else's life was up to us. Honestly, I know the ones we kill are better off. I've seen Tyson make grown men cry and beg for their lives. Those are usually their last words.

"Maybe I should just let you guys handle all of them. It'd make my life easier," Tyson says in thought.

"Nah, that's half the fun." Ryat slaps him on the back.

He's got to be a Lord. He wouldn't be here if he wasn't. He doesn't seem like an errand bitch boy to Tyson. So that's not an option. He had called him Ty. They have to be close. And he's not wearing a Blackout security T-shirt. I look over his white hoodie and dark-wash jeans. He doesn't dress in a suit like Tyson does, but that doesn't mean shit. As far as I know, a Lord can be anyone. They strategically place them where they best fit in the world, whether it be the fucking president or an owner of a bar in a sketchy area.

"Any problems?" Tyson asks, cutting the zip tie on the man's wrists and flipping him over onto his back.

"There was a girl." His head snaps up to look at me when I speak. "He had his daughter with him."

His blue eyes dart around the room. "Well, where the fuck is she?" he demands.

"Told you we should have brought her." Alex gives me a fuck you smile. He wants someone else in the doghouse with Tyson other than himself for once.

"I wasn't going to let her be killed because her father is an idiot." I point at him, lying on the metal table. "I stuck her. Finn placed her body in the car they arrived in. She'll wake up in a few hours and not remember shit." The drugs he provides us with are some powerful ones. We've never used them on ourselves, but they drop a three-hundred-pound man like a drunk girl's underwear. With how small she was, she could be out the rest of the night. And the side effects could cause loss of memory. I'm guessing on that one. They never live long enough to tell us. "Plus," I add. "We had our masks on. Too much was happening for her to even retain any information to lead her back to us."

He nods. "You better hope so." Then he looks over at Finn. "I'm guessing she gave you that shiner?"

He reaches up and touches his face, hissing in a breath. "The bitch punched me."

Ryat walks over to the guy, looking over him. "This is the president of Oakley's Bank."

Tyson nods.

"He's been grooming his daughter for years," Ryat states with a heavy sigh.

"Yeah, he's a sick bastard," Tyson adds. "He's been forcing her into a world that she should have never known existed." He looks up at us. "If she comes for you guys, you'll have your hands full. She won't go down as easily the second time."

"Meaning?" Alex asks, wanting clarification he can just kill her if there's a next time.

Tyson smirks. "Meaning they don't call her wicked for nothing."

Finn snorts. "She was a crazy fucking bitch."

"They always are." Jenks agrees.

"Yeah." Tyson pulls a pair of gloves out of a box and lays them on the table next to the guy while he rolls up the sleeves of his dark-gray button-up. "But they're the only ones worth having."

We wrap up what Tyson needs, and an hour later, we're walking into the house. I make my way upstairs and decide to go by her room. Opening the door, I see she's passed out in bed, and Tatum is asleep next to her. Some woman is on her TV screen that hangs on the wall running through the woods screaming while a man chases her down with a machete.

I walk over to Raylee's side of the bed and see four bottles of wine. Two are on her nightstand, the others on the bed. All empty. I smile because I bet she thought of me while she was drinking those.

Her phone lights up next to her, and I pick it up to see it's a text from Nate. Grinding my teeth, I open it.

Nate: *I'm sorry, Ray. Please call me. I need to talk to you.*

I delete the text and read over the last several he's sent her. She's ignoring him. *Good girl.* He doesn't deserve a second of her time. Deleting the rest, I shut it off and place it back where I found it.

I run my knuckles over her cheek, pushing some blond strands off her face, then lean down, whispering in her ear. "I'll take care of him, princess." Then I exit her room to go take a shower and get some rest. I have to be up early in the morning because Tyson needs us back at Blackout.

RAYLEE

TATUM AND I pull up to Mike's house Sunday night, and she sighs heavily. I feel rested, almost like a new me. After we had several bottles of wine last night, we passed out in my bed. My body was exhausted along with my mind. I woke up this morning to find myself home alone, other than Tatum next to me, and was thankful for that. When you live with four guys, it can be overwhelming. Thankfully, most of them keep to themselves. They only ever bother me if Colt tells them to.

"You sure you're okay being here?" Tatum asks, breaking the silence between us.

"Yep." I nod once. I don't give a fuck what people think about me. Clearly.

She scrolls on her phone for a few seconds and then looks at me. "The video is gone."

"Doubtful," I disagree and pull down the visor to reapply my lipstick. "It's there somewhere, I'm sure."

My cell dings, and I see it's a text from Nate. Rolling my eyes, I turn the ringer off.

"What did it say?" she asks, watching me throw it into the back seat.

I won't be needing that tonight. "Don't know. Don't care." I woke up with it off this morning and guessed it had died at some point last night, so I haven't been on it much today.

She pats my shoulder. "I still can't believe Colt posted that shit online. That was over the line. Even for him."

I don't keep any secrets from Tatum. She knows what I've done with Colt over the years, especially that night with all of them after he stopped recording me. But who knows how many times he's done that? How many videos he has just sitting and waiting to be used. "Why did you go to the party?" I ask her, changing the subject. I know it wasn't to see her brother—they fight like cats and dogs. She wasn't mad at me when I told her I slept with Alex, just grossed out.

"Billy didn't want to go to the movies. When I told him that I wanted to spend time with you, he suggested going to Colt's party. That I would get to see you when you got home."

I nod and watch the kids partying on the front lawn of the Williams home. I went to high school with Mike and his twin brother Mitch when my mom and I moved here. Their parents are loaded, of course. So any chance they have to throw a party at their parents' mansion, they take it. They must be out of town this weekend.

Mike and I have a history, but I'm not ashamed of it. It is what it is. Plus, if Mike hadn't started fucking me and ran out like a little bitch when I got blood on his dick, who knows if Colt would have stepped in and shown me how it's done.

"What are you going to do when you see Billy here with her?" I ask, changing the subject again. We're only here because she wants to track down her boyfriend and see if the rumors she heard are true.

"I'm ... I'm not sure." She gives a rough laugh. "I guess it depends on if I'm drunk by then or not."

"You know he's going to marry her, right?" I hate to break her heart, but he's been on and off with Cheryl since before I moved in with the Knoxes our sophomore year in high school. He cheats, she cheats, but they always go back to one another.

"Probably," she agrees. "I saw the red flags before we even started dating."

"You and me both." I snort, referring to how I still allow Colt to fuck me. "We're both color blind."

She laughs and nods. "Ain't that the truth."

Tatum and Billy have a toxic relationship. The only difference between her and Billy, and Colt and me is that we actually do hate one another.

"She kept blowing up his phone Friday night at the party." She glances at her cell and then tosses it into the back seat with mine.

"What was she saying to him?" I wonder.

"That she was sorry." Tatum huffs.

"About what exactly? He was the one who dumped her last."

She shrugs. "No clue, and he wouldn't tell me when I asked." Running her hand through her hair, she pushes the dark strands away from her face and smiles over at me. "How about we find out?"

I nod. "I'm ready when you are."

She pushes the passenger door open and gets out. I smile, doing the same, needing some excitement. I'm a ride-or-die friend to the end. So if she starts throwing punches, I'll jump right in and throw mine, no questions asked.

The house sits on twelve acres tucked back behind a tree line. It's dark gray with black shutters, white columns, and a wraparound porch. It's two stories and has a section referred to as the guest wing. I don't think anyone ever uses it. Mrs. Williams keeps the property fully staffed at all times.

"In The End" by Black Veil Brides blares from the speakers when we enter the house. I instantly feel eyes on me. It's the sex tape. Friday night at my house, I went straight to my room after I set Colt's car on fire and then Nate showed up, so I never had to face anyone. Now I'm not only a slut but also crazy because of the stunt I pulled with his car.

Tatum gets my attention, sliding her arm in the crook of mine and raises her chin, noticing the way conversations die down around us. "They just wish their friend was as cool as mine," she states, giving me a big smile.

I laugh. "Come on. Let's get our drink on. Something tells me we're both going to need it."

We enter the kitchen, and I see Mitch standing at the large bar, mixing drinks. "Hey, ladies," he calls out, seeing us.

Mitch Williams has always been a cool guy. Nothing like his brother.

He comes around the bar and gives us both a hug. "What's been going on? What can I get you two to drink?"

"Dude, don't act like you haven't watched her sex tape." A guy I've never seen before throws his arm over Mitch's shoulders and winks at me. "Maybe the three of us can make one tonight."

"Shut up, Joe." Mitch shoves him away and grabs a couple of shot glasses. "Show some respect."

Joe snorts. "You don't respect whores."

I flinch at his words but try to look unaffected by tucking a piece of my hair behind my ear.

"Ignore him." Mitch gives us a smirk, pouring some vodka into the glasses. "Drink up, ladies." He places them in front of us.

We both down them without question. Hissing in a breath, Tatum twirls her finger around in the air. "Keep 'em coming."

"Uh-oh." He pours two more. "Anything I can help with?" he asks, setting them in front of us as well.

"Nope." She throws hers back, and I swallow mine.

"The night has just begun, ladies." He grabs a couple of red Solo cups to make us actual drinks, and then hands me one of the cups. "Still drink Malibu and pineapple?" he asks.

Smiling, I take it from him. "I do. Thank you." I used to spend lots of time at this house partying. Taking a sip, I put the cup down and ask, "Where's your brother?" Might as well get this over with. He'll have something to say about the video. And I'm sure it'll piss me off. I'd prefer to throw my drink on him now rather than later.

He starts laughing while pouring Tatum's drink. "In jail."

"What?" Tatum gasps.

I chuckle, taking another sip. "Why am I not surprised?"

"Yeah, he got picked up yesterday. Since Mom and Dad are out of town for a few days, I'm pretending that I don't know he's locked up. I'll get him out tomorrow morning," he adds. "That way I know he can't crash my party."

"Thank God," I mumble around my cup.

Mike and Mitch are very different people. They look identical—pretty, dark blue eyes, light brown hair that they both keep short on the sides and longer on top. But they dress different. Mitch has always been more preppy and makes sure he's ready for anything. Whereas Mike would show up to school like he just rolled out of bed. They're the exact opposite of one another. Mitch got straight A's, while Mike barely graduated high school. I never really cared for Mike. I only went to his party that night five years ago because Colt told me I couldn't. I snuck out of the house. I still don't know how he found out I came here and what Mike and I did. I just wanted to fit in. It was hard being Colt's stepsister who everyone ignored. Mike actually gave me the time of day that night, so when he led me up to his room, I didn't think twice about it.

"Can you make mine a double?" Tatum asks, watching him mix her drink.

"That rough, huh?" he asks.

"Raylee? Tatum?" I hear a familiar female voice from behind us. We both spin around to see Raven entering the kitchen underneath a man's arm.

As usual, she looks gorgeous. She's a petite thing. Can't be more than five-two without her heels on. She has her dyed-black hair pulled up and away from her face in a high ponytail. She wears a white dress that shows off her massive boobs, and black heels. Her parents got divorced our senior year in high school. Her mother wanted to get fake boobs to celebrate the settlement. She won but didn't want to get them done alone, so she bought Raven a pair too.

Back where I grew up, that would be insane. Parents didn't buy their young kids plastic surgery. But here? This town is full of rich kids who get whatever they want at the drop of a hat. Girls were getting their noses done as young as sophomore year.

"Hey, girl." I open my arms to hug her when she pushes the man away.

"Haven't seen you ladies in a while." She pulls away to hug Tatum.

"Yeah, I haven't seen you over at the house."

Raven is Alex's on-again off-again girlfriend. They've been together since our junior year in high school. She's just as crazy as he is. Rumor has it he killed someone over her. I can't say I believe it, but it wouldn't surprise me. I once watched him hit a guy in the head with a beer bottle because the man smacked her ass.

"Yes, well, let me introduce you to Rick." She points over at the guy standing beside her. Clearly telling me the reason she hasn't been at the house is because her and Alex are currently off.

I've always liked Raven. She's not afraid to get her hands dirty. Tatum and I went out with her last summer, and she got us banned from a bar. Picking a fight with the owner's daughter will do the trick. But to be fair, none of us started it. The bitch jumped Raven, and we couldn't just stand by and not help a friend out.

I go to reach out my hand to Rick, but he pulls me in for a hug, his hand a little too low on my ass for my liking, so I push him off.

He goes to hug Tatum, and she takes a step back from him.

"We have to get together soon," Raven speaks.

Her date's phone rings, and he pulls it out of his pocket to answer. "Be right back," he tells her and turns around, exiting the kitchen.

"Who are you dating?" Tatum beats me to it.

"I met him through my mom," she answers, adjusting her dress to make sure her boobs are on display.

"Your mom?" Tatum pulls her lip back. "How old is he?"

"Thirty-three." She winks, smiling. "No more playing around with boys."

"Gross," Tatum whispers. "He was like ten years old when you were born."

Raven laughs. "Date up, ladies. I promise. You'll like it."

I look at the guy, and he's talking to another girl, his eyes clearly on her chest. "He's checking that girl out," I tell her.

I'm not one of those friends who will keep secrets from you. If I know something, I'm telling you. You can hate me all you want after you take your sleazy, cheating boyfriend back, but at least I know you're aware of the situation.

"We're not exclusive." She waves it off. "It's just for fun."

"You ready, Raven?" he asks, coming back over to us. "Let's get the fuck out of here and go to a real party."

I don't know what it is about him, but I'm not a fan.

"Yeah." She pulls us both in for a hug. "Call me. We'll get together."

They turn and walk out just as someone else catches my eye. Billy enters the kitchen with none other than Cheryl under his arm. They're technically supposed to be broken up right now. He's been dating Tatum for a month.

I clear my throat and nudge her arm. When she notices him, I feel her body stiffen beside me. "Motherfucker," she hisses under her breath. "I fucking knew it."

"What?" Mitch looks up, his eyes darting around the room to see what's going on. He doesn't tolerate fights in this house. He'll be the first to knock a guy out just to break it up.

Billy has his back toward us, talking to a couple of guys over by the entrance. My eyes drop to see Cheryl's hand in his back pocket, and I quickly down my drink. I'm pissed that I don't even get to enjoy it.

Tatum storms off, and I set my empty cup down, wiping some off my chin. "Refill, please." Then I take off after Tatum.

She walks up to him and taps his shoulder. He turns around with a smile on his face, but it drops the moment he sees her.

"Tatum?" He pushes Cheryl off him. "What the fuck are you doing here?"

"What am I doing here? What the fuck are you doing here?" She stabs his chest. "And with her?"

Cheryl averts her brown eyes because she knows damn well that Billy and Tatum have been dating. But who am I to say anything? I fucked Colt while I was with Nate.

"Tatum, let's take this outside." Billy grabs her arm.

"No." She shoves him off. "We can talk about it right here."

His eyes narrow down on her. "I'm nothing like your best friend."

"What the fuck does that mean?" she yells.

He steps up to her, and I square my shoulders. "It means I don't want everyone to know our business."

"Then maybe you shouldn't parade around two different parties with two different women back-to-back," I offer. Because why not? I never learned how to not be a smart-ass. It comes naturally.

His eyes go to mine, and he scoffs. "Maybe you should keep your legs closed."

Tatum gasps and slaps him across the face. Billy bumps his chest into hers, and I shove him away from her.

"Guys. Guys. Calm down." Mitch intervenes, pulling Billy away from us.

"I don't know what this looks like, but—"

"What it looks like is you're cheating on me," Tatum interrupts Billy.

Cheryl throws her hands up in the air and all but runs out of the kitchen. I'm surprised when Billy doesn't go after her.

"Babe." He pushes off Mitch and walks over to her. "I love you. I'm with you. Why would I be with her?"

She crosses her arms over her chest. "You really expect me to believe that shit?" Shaking her head, she adds, "I'm done," and goes to walk off, but he grabs her hand, pulling her to a stop.

"Please?" he begs. "Just let me take you home. We can talk." He lifts his eyes and looks around the room for I don't know what before they fall back to hers. "I'll tell you anything you want to know. I'll show you my phone."

I don't like how he said he'll tell her *anything* she wants to know instead of *everything*. It saves him from having to tell on himself. One of those, if you don't ask, you don't need to know situations. His way of controlling what he tells her. Rolling my eyes, I say, "Texts and pictures can be deleted."

He ignores me. "Please, babe? I'm begging you. Just give me this."

"You don't owe him anything," I tell her.

She hangs her head, and I know I've lost. She's getting ready to leave with him, but I get it. This is Colt and me. Back and forth. Every fucking day. It's literally the definition of insanity. Doing the same thing over and over, expecting a different result. I have bruises and scars to prove it. Some of us will choose stupidity over rational thought when it comes to good dick.

"It's okay. I'll be fine," I tell her, placing my hand on her shoulder. I won't make her feel guilty if she wants to leave with him tonight. She deserves answers. Even if she finds out they're lies two months down the road.

She lifts her head and narrows her eyes on him. "I'll only leave with you if you apologize to Raylee."

"Oh, that's not—"

"I'm sorry." He looks my way, interrupting me. "I shouldn't have said that. That was uncalled for, and I'm sorry."

You could hear a pin drop. There isn't even any music playing in the background. Just an awkward silence. And all eyes are on us. I nod once. "Thank you." I'm not apologizing for what I said to him because that was the truth. Don't want to get caught cheating? Don't flaunt your side bitch around.

He holds his hand out to her, and she takes a step back. "I'll meet you out in the car. I need a second with Raylee."

He nods and turns, walking out of the kitchen, and hushed voices start back up again while "vicious" by Tate McRae starts to play. She turns to face me. "I'm so sorry, but—"

"Hey, don't apologize." I wave her off. "I just hope you keep an open mind. Don't let him gaslight you. Don't let him talk you back into a relationship until he tells you everything."

"I won't. Promise." She pulls me in for a hug. "Love you, Ray." And then she too is leaving the party.

I make my way back over to the bar where Mitch is now standing again. He hands me another drink. "I made this one stronger."

"Thanks," I mumble. I'm already starting to feel those two shots and the last drink I had.

"You can hang with me," he offers.

"Sounds good." I'll leave after this. Not like there's anyone else here who I want to visit with. I'll finish this drink, get an Uber, and then go home and take a nice hot bath before locking myself in my room. Maybe watch a movie on Netflix. I'll have Tatum bring me back to get my car in the morning.

"Ray? May I speak to you?"

The cup pauses halfway to my mouth when I hear his voice behind me. Mitch looks over my shoulder and then back at me, frowning.

I sigh and turn around to face Nate. "There's nothing to say," I inform him.

I understand that others won't agree with what I like. Or what I want. But fuck him. He made me feel ashamed of what I like, and that's unacceptable. "Thanks for the drinks, Mitch," I say and walk off.

"Anytime," he calls out.

I'm making my way through the living room when someone grabs my arm and yanks me to a stop. "Fuck." I hiss, trying not to spill my drink at the motion.

I spin around to see Nate has followed me. "What do you want?" I snap.

He places his hands in the front pockets of his jeans. "I've been trying to get ahold of you."

"I've been ignoring you for a reason."

His eyes narrow, and he takes a step toward me, closing the small space between us. "I don't know why you're being a bitch."

"Me?" I gasp.

"Yes, you. You're the one who was cheating on me." He removes his hands from his pockets and points at himself. "With your stepbrother," Nate spits out with disgust.

"Look." I push my hip out. "When I care enough to talk about this, I'll call you." Giving him my back, I go to leave but he grabs my arm again and yanks me back this time while spinning me around.

"You're leaving with me. Now." He growls in my face.

I laugh, shaking my head. He's got to be joking. "I'm not going anywhere with you, Nate. It's over. We're over."

His fingers dig into my arm, causing me to hiss in a breath before he starts dragging me out of the living room. Thankfully, the place is packed, so he has a hard time getting us through the crowd. I manage to jerk my arm free, and he spins back around to grab me again.

"I'm not fucking playing with you, Ray!" he snaps in my face.

"What the fuck—?" My words cut off when I see a set of green eyes watching me from across the living room. Colt is here with his *besties* and Mitch. What the fuck is he doing with them?

All their eyes are on me. My teeth grind when Colt leans in to whisper something to Alex. He nods, and then the three of them take off, leaving Colt there with Mitch, who then walks off as well. He's just staring at me. A look that I know all too well. My body breaks out in goose bumps, and I swallow nervously. Heat rushes up my spine, and I blame it on the shots I downed. I have got to get the fuck out of here. And quick.

I look up at Nate and growl. "I need to use the restroom," I lie. Now I have to figure out how to hide from two men.

He removes his hand from my arm. "You have five minutes."

I refrain from laughing at that and spin around, making a mad dash to the front door, getting the hell out of here.

Seven

COLTON

I GRIP HER upper arm and yank her out of the living room.

"Hey—" she protests, trying to dig her heels into the floor, but I drag her into a nearby room and shove her in, slamming the door shut behind me and flipping on the light. "What the fuck are you doing?" she demands, whirling around on me.

"What in the fuck are you doing?" I growl.

"Trying to leave, but since that's not happening…" She lifts the red Solo cup to her mouth and takes a big gulp.

"No, with Nate. What the fuck were you doing with Nate?" I came thinking Mike would give her shit, but I overheard a few guys talking out back by the pool when we first arrived that he wasn't going to be here tonight. Then when I saw her talking to Nate, it pissed me off. He showed his true colors after he watched the video. He no longer gets to be around her. Which is why I released it in the first place—to run him off. I'm not letting him get close again. Not in the way he'd like anyway.

She had been ignoring his texts. Did she talk to him today? "Did you come here with him?" I demand. I saw him touch her, and I didn't like it one fucking bit. I couldn't hear what they were saying from across the room with the loud music, but she didn't seem very happy with him. When I asked Mitch what the fuck was going on between them, he said she had acted surprised to see Nate here. But that still doesn't explain why he was dragging her out of the living room and where the fuck they were going.

She places one hand on her hip and takes another drink from her Solo cup, obviously going to ignore my question.

I rip it from her hand, making some spill down the front of her dress, and set it on the dresser to my right.

"Hey, I was drinking that," she protests. "What's wrong, Colt? Are you jealous?" Her red lips turn up in the corners before she starts laughing at the stupid accusation.

I grab her dress and yank her to me. Spinning her around, I shove her back into the wall next to the closed door. Our faces are so close that if I stuck my tongue out, I could lick the liquor off her chin that I spilled. "Goddamn right, I'm jealous," I growl.

Her laughter dies down, and her lips part on a sharp intake of breath.

My eyes roam all over her perfect face. She reminds me of a doll. Slender neck, defined jaw with a petite heart-shaped face, and those crystal-blue eyes that make me weak in the knees any time I look at them. Fuck, my cock is hard just thinking about making her face dirty. She's got a lot of makeup on tonight. Her lips painted that signature red color that looks so good smeared around my cock. Her eyes are lined in thick black liner with matching mascara. I imagine smearing my cum all over it, watching it all run down her face while she gasps for air.

"Are you going to make me prove a point, princess?" I ask, getting back on track. I'll get what I want. Very soon.

She licks her lips, her brows pulling together in confusion. "A point?"

Cute. "Yeah, that you belong to me." No matter who she's brought home—Raylee Adams belongs to me. She always has. From the moment she stepped into my father's house, I claimed her.

She swallows nervously, her hands coming up and gripping my forearms as I keep her pinned to the wall, biding my time. I need to get her worked up. As if she's not already. I saw the way she looked at me across the living room. Raylee can be a bitch, but she's also very readable. I know every little sound that mouth can make. I know every move her body has. And I know just how to make her beg for me.

"Maybe that's what you want?" I question, breaking her silence. She's scared and unsure how to react to me right now. Good. I like to keep her guessing. "To prove to everyone here that you're mine."

I barely hear her argument. "No." The single word makes her body tremble against mine.

"I think so." I reach up and run my hand through her soft curls. She wore it how I like it. All down and in big waves. It tangles easier when she's got product in it. I love to mess it up. "I already have an idea on how to do that."

"Id-idea?" She shifts from foot to foot.

"I'll put a collar around your neck." My eyes drop to it and see her swallow nervously. "And I'll lead you around this party by a leash." She whimpers, closing her eyes, and I watch her dark lashes fan her cheeks. "Naked, on all fours with your face covered in my spit and my cum dripping out of your cunt."

Her eyes spring open and are wide, lips parting on a small gasp, looking shocked by what I just said. Nothing should surprise her, and by the way she presses her hips into mine, I know she's visualizing it right now.

I let go of her hair and run my knuckles down over her neck, feeling her pulse racing. My girl is all worked up now. Just as I expected, it didn't take much. "Is that what you want, princess? Want me to humiliate you in front of everyone?"

She doesn't answer. Her wide eyes just search mine while her breathing picks up. She knows I'm not joking. I never do when it comes to Raylee.

"See..." I drop my hands to the hem of her short dress. Slowly, I pull it up, letting my knuckles graze her skin in the process. Once it gets to her waist, I let go and push her thong to the side, running my fingers over her pussy. She's wet and makes no attempt to stop me. "I think you want me to degrade you and show them what a filthy slut you are." I had Finn shorten that video before posting it online. It was only ten seconds long of her on her knees in the formal dining room sucking my dick. These men and women here have no idea just how dirty she likes it.

"Colt," she whimpers my name, her heavy eyes falling shut once again.

I push a finger into her. "You'll be unsatisfied, of course. Because I want them to watch you beg me to get you off. I want them to watch you cry, let them see how desperate you get..." I pause, slipping a second finger into her. I feel her knees start to buckle, and I wrap my free hand around her throat to help hold her up against the wall. "When your body is desperate for a release."

"Please," she begs, her voice trembling like her body while her hips start to gently rock against my hand.

"Please what, princess?" My thumb runs over her clit just slightly, knowing she wants me to play with it.

Her hands come up to my jeans, and she fumbles with the zipper. I smile in victory, removing my hand from between her legs, forcing a growl of frustration from her lips. "Please fuck me—"

She's interrupted by the door opening beside us. Alex pops his head in and winks at me. "Ready."

I nod. "We'll be right there."

Closing the door behind him, he leaves us alone once again.

She sags against the wall, now panting and all worked up. Ready to be fucked.

Reaching out, I pick up her drink that I placed on the dresser to my left and hold it up to her lips. "Drink up," I order, pressing it to her lips.

She tilts her head back, and I force her to drink all of it. Some runs down the sides of her mouth, but her throat works while she swallows. Once I hear it's gone, I toss the cup to the side, and she's gasping for air.

I push some blond strands back from her perfectly dolled-up face. Leaning in, I lick up her neck, tasting the pineapple juice and Malibu Rum that missed her mouth. "Remember what you just begged for, princess. Because you're going to get it." Then I yank her dress back down and grab her arm, pulling her out of the room.

RAYLEE

MY EYES DART around the hallways and rooms while I allow Colt to drag me through the party. My heart hammers in my chest, and I can't catch my breath. My underwear is soaked, and I can feel a breeze on my ass where he didn't pull my dress down far enough.

He wants to humiliate me in front of all these people. I like the fact that I am not responsible. It turns me on to know that I'm just an object, and I have no obligation to try to keep up appearances. I'm no longer Raylee Lexington Adams. I'm just his—Colt's slut. I enjoy the place he drags me to when I cry and beg him for any kind of pleasure.

If anyone knew how I really felt, they'd probably put me in therapy. Or a padded room in a straitjacket.

I always had this desire to be owned. Some people would call that lack of self-respect. I say fuck them. It's not a crime to be a sexual person. Smokers crave a cigarette. Druggies crave their next fix. And me? I crave dick. It just so happens to be my stepbrother's. No one else has ever treated me like he does. Or gotten me off like him. I swear, the guy could train my body to come at the sound of a single word if he wanted to. But that wouldn't be any fun for him. He'd never want it to be that easy for me. It's frustrating, to say the least.

"MIDDLE OF THE NIGHT" by Elley Duhé plays as he brings me through the living room and blood starts rushing in my ears. *This is it.* He's going to make me undress in front of all these people, get on all fours, and parade me around like a show dog. The thought makes my thighs tighten.

No one pays any attention to us as he leads me to the other side of the living room and out a back door. I look around to see people jumping in the pool. Some sitting in lawn chairs. There's a firepit where others are roasting marshmallows.

He takes me across the backyard, and I see the in-law suite. I stumble over my heels, but he keeps me upright. Shit, is it the alcohol or because I'm nervous? Maybe both.

"Colt, what are we doing out here?" I ask softly. "That's Mike's house," I tell him as if he doesn't already know.

Mike has been in trouble for the past few years. He didn't even graduate from Barrington. He made it to his junior year with Colt and the guys and then got kicked out. His parents made him move into the in-law suite that sits on the back of their property when they found out about it.

"Colt?" He doesn't answer me. "We shouldn't be out here." No one is allowed out here when the twins throw a party. Everyone knows it's off-limits and always has been. Even back when we were in high school.

We reach the front door, and he turns the knob before pushing me inside. I immediately turn around and go to exit but run right into Colt, making me squeal in surprise.

"Shh." He wraps his arms around me, holding me to his chest.

My hands dig into the soft material of his T-shirt, knowing I can't escape this. He's made up his mind. He wants to humiliate me, and this is how he plans to do it. I don't get to choose how he makes me his slut. And the biggest part of me likes that. That's what turns me on—having no choice.

After gently kissing my hair, Colt pries himself away from me and grabs my hand, then he turns me to face our audience.

I look over the house. I've never been in here before. There are not many decorations. White walls with white leather furniture. Light gray tiled floor. It's got an open kitchen area to the left. But other than that, it's more of a mancave.

Back in the right corner is a bed with one nightstand and a dresser. A pool table sits to the right with a dartboard on the wall and a set of stairs that leads to a loft. But it looks unfinished right now. The construction equipment that lays around confirms my thoughts.

Once I've looked at everything else in the room, my eyes finally fall to the guests. Alex stands with his arms crossed over his chest and his eyes on mine. Finn stands next to him, playing with his damn knife. Jenks stands to the far left of them, typing away on his phone. And then my eyes fall on the chair between them. Nate sits in it. He's glaring at me.

I feel hands on my shoulders, and I jump.

"Calm down, princess." Colt leans down and kisses my cheek. "Nate here has been talking about you tonight."

"What was he saying?" Frowning, I ask Colt as if Nate isn't right in front of me.

"That you're a fucking whore," Nate snaps. He goes to get out of the chair, but Alex grips his hair and forces him back down into the seat, making a growl come from his pursed lips. I realize his hands are behind his back when he shakes his upper body, trying to get loose with no success. They must have restrained him.

"I … I don't understand," I say, my hands shaking. "You were just trying to force me to leave with you." I take a step closer to Nate.

Colt's body stiffens. "He was?"

I nod, swallowing. "Yes. He grabbed my arm." I hold it out, and just as I expected, there's already a bruise forming where Nate had ahold of it. "He was trying to drag me out of the house. Said that we were leaving together."

"That's … interesting." Colt gives a laugh that holds no humor.

108

"She's lying!" Nate yells. "You're going to believe her? She's a fucking liar."

Colt snorts, and his eyes meet mine. "Raylee is a lot of things, but she doesn't lie. Do you, princess?"

I shake my head. "Why would I lie about that? I've been ignoring you. I told you it was over and that I want nothing to do with you."

Nate shakes his head quickly and looks over at Colt. "She begged me. Begged me to take her home—"

Alex punches Nate in the side of his face, shutting him up. "I've heard enough of that," he states, rubbing his knuckles.

Colt arches a brow at me, and I shake my head. The need to explain myself has me licking my lips nervously. "That's not true. I never ..."

Reaching up, he wraps his hand around my neck, and I trail off. His green eyes search mine before he smiles. "I know he's lying."

I let out a shaky breath. I'm not sure why I care that Colt believes me. Maybe it's more the fact of him not believing Nate.

Colt tilts his head to the side in thought. "I think he's just confused. What do you think, boys?"

"Definitely," Finn agrees.

"He's obviously never seen her beg," Alex adds, making Jenks and Finn laugh.

"Let's show him." Colt releases my neck and steps back from me.

His words make my stomach turn in the best way. I hate that it excites me. *This is wrong.* I shake my head. "We shouldn't—"

"Come here," Colt orders, and his voice seems to boom through the quiet, little house. He's now standing by the couch across from the chair where Nate sits and the others stand.

My pussy tightens at the command in his voice. All business. He knows I can't deny that. Fuck, I hate him so much. Tears prick my eyes that he puts me in these situations that I crave. Why can't another guy do this? Why couldn't Nate have been this way? Or any other man on this planet, for that matter?

"Don't make me say it again, princess," Colt warns.

My feet move on their own, walking over a plush white rug to stand in front of him. My head hangs low, staring at the black heels I chose to wear tonight. I almost wore tennis shoes, thinking that my feet would hurt. Little did I know they'd be the least of my worries.

He puts his finger under my chin and lifts my head to where I must look up at him. A single tear runs down my cheek.

"Crying already?" he asks with a smirk on his lips. My hands itch to slap his pretty-boy face.

He said he'd make me a sobbing mess, begging for a release. I believed every word he had said. Maybe this was his plan all along. I thought he meant in front of everyone at the party, but he meant in front of my ex.

Reaching out, he grips my chin. His fingers dig into my skin, forcing a whimper from my parted lips. Holding me in place, he lowers his face to mine. "I love it when you cry," he whispers before running the tip of his tongue along my face, tasting my tear that had just fallen. "It makes my cock hard."

My eyes fall shut, and the room feels like it's tilting. The last drink Colt made me down must be hitting me. About time.

I feel his hot breath on my face as he moves to my ear. He starts nibbling on it, forcing a shiver out of me. "What are you, princess?" he growls in my ear.

"Your slut," I answer breathlessly, so easily falling into that role that he's taught me to crave.

"And what are you going to do for me?" His lips trail down to my neck as he tilts my head to the side by my chin.

"Anything," I respond desperately.

"You're such a good girl," he praises, and my legs tremble at the thought of pleasing him.

I love when he calls me that almost as much as his slut.

He pulls away and lets go of me, making me feel cold. Before he walks off, he commands, "Get undressed and sit on the couch."

Eight

COLTON

I LIED, BUT she didn't catch it. I didn't know if Nate was talking shit about her to his friends, but the sorry bastard told on himself like I was hoping he would. I can't figure out why he'd want to leave the party with her. Where would he have taken her? That video of her and me humiliated him to his friends. Everyone who's watched it assumes it was recent. Since they started dating. So him trying to get her to leave with him has me questioning just what the fuck he was up to with my girl.

I go over to the table that sits in the kitchen area. Mike's parents are renovating the upstairs loft, which means the construction workers are leaving shit all over the place. I had the guys gather some things that we could use. This place couldn't be more perfect for what I'm about to do to Raylee.

When I saw her talking to Nate, I knew I had to do something. Then Mitch came up to me, asking if everything was okay. I always liked him. We got along easily. He knew to stay the fuck away from Raylee. And he knew that I couldn't just let Nate touch my girl like that in front of everyone at his party. He told me to do what I needed to but to use Mike's house. Where no one would find us.

Picking up what I need, I turn and lean against the table, watching her. She silently undresses, standing in front of the couch. Reaching down, she grips the hem of her dress and pulls it up and over her head. She sucks her stomach in, showing her ribs as she takes a deep breath before tossing it to the side. Her curled hair falls down over her breasts, and I have the urge to tell her to pull it up and out of the way but refrain.

She goes to sit down, thinking she's done, when I speak. "Thong too." She pauses and looks at me. "Naked."

Biting her bottom lip, she only hesitates for a second before she grips the lace sides and pushes them down her long, lean legs, and places it on the coffee table. Sitting down, she slips her right foot out of her heels.

"Leave those on," I say, and she nods, slipping her foot back into it.

"You guys are fucking sick," Nate spits out. "I'm not going to watch this shit! She was my girlfriend!" he yells, his face going red.

I grab a roll of duct tape off the table and toss it over to Alex, who catches it midair. "You'll talk when we tell you to," I say.

Nate tries to fight them, but Finn grabs his hair, holding him in place while Alex takes the duct tape and wraps it around his head a few times before tearing it off and tossing it onto the coffee table.

I wait to see if Raylee says anything, but she doesn't. Instead, her eyes drop to what I hold in my hand, and her breathing picks up. Pushing off the table, I walk over to the side of the couch so I don't block Nate's view of her. I push her bleach blond hair off her chest so I can see her tits. I slide my hand down her sternum, watching her nipples harden at the simple touch and her body silently begging me for more.

"What do you say?" I ask, lowering my hand over her stomach.

"Please?" she whispers.

I drop what's in my hand and grip her hair, yanking her head back so she has to look up at me hovering over her. "I didn't hear you. What does a slut do, princess?"

"She begs," she answers, sucking in a deep breath.

I get to her lower abdomen, and she spreads her legs wider for me. I smile, bringing my hand to a stop and pulling it back up her body, making her growl in frustration. When it gets to her neck, I wrap my fingers around it and squeeze. "What are you waiting for?"

"Please?" Her voice rises just a bit with a little more desperation than before but still not enough.

I sigh in disappointment. "I guess if you're not going to use your voice, then I'll take it away."

"No. No." She tries to rise up on the couch but goes nowhere. "Please?" she asks, her hands fisting the couch on either side of her. "Please, I need it." New tears spring to her gorgeous eyes. "I need you."

"Need me to what?" I want Nate to hear her say it.

"Let me come."

God, she's fucking perfect. I spent the first year hating her because I wanted her so bad and knew I couldn't have her. Then I did, and it made things even worse. My hatred grew for her every time I heard someone say her name. She was fucking everywhere. My home. My school. She walked into my life and turned it all upside down.

It's not like we've fucked every day for the past six years. There were times when we'd go months without so much as a hello when we crossed paths in the halls at home.

That first year when I was at Barrington and she was still living with her mom and my dad was excruciating. I imagined her fucking all those high school guys. It was like taking away a child's favorite toy. I still had eyes and ears at the school for me, but it was different. I couldn't physically see what was going on with her.

We had a family dinner night twice a month and I'd make sure to remind her who she belonged to after our parents went to bed. But it still wasn't enough. I couldn't take it.

Then she finally graduated, and my father got her into Barrington University. That's when I knew I had to have her in my house. I had to make her just as miserable as she made me.

Now I realize I could have had her this way every day. I should have made her mine sooner.

I look over to Nate sitting in the chair. His brown eyes are narrowed to slits, and what part of his face I can see that's not duct-taped is red with embarrassment.

"Did Nate ever get you off, princess?" I wonder out loud, already knowing this answer. She tells Tatum everything. Sometimes I hear their conversations when she's over at the house visiting, or when they're talking on the phone. Other times, I read her texts while she sleeps.

She whimpers but answers softly, "No."

"Did you fake it every time?" I also know this answer.

"Yes." She tries to pull away because I'm still holding her head back, making her look up at the ceiling. But I don't let go.

Nate's shaking his head while sitting in the chair, but I ignore him, looking down at her. She's crying, tears running down both sides of her face.

I let go of her, and she softly cries when I take a step back from her. I spot her underwear on the coffee table and get an idea. "Finn, why don't you pour me a drink."

He nods and makes his way over to the kitchen area, and I hear him fixing one while I watch her squirm in place. "Place your hands behind your back," I order.

She lowers her head, sniffing, and pulls her arms behind her. I grab what I dropped and cross her wrists, securing the zip tie around them. Tight enough to pinch her skin. I want her to suffer tonight in the best way. I want her to have marks once I'm done with her.

"Here you go." Finn sets a glass of scotch on the table and then goes back to his spot by the chair.

I pick up her thong and turn them inside out. "Look how wet I got you," I say, holding them up to her.

She lifts her head and looks at them. Then her eyes slowly meet mine.

"What did I say to get you so worked up, princess?"

Her eyes widen, and she shakes her head. I give her a smile, and her shoulders start to shake. "Colt … please?"

"I didn't tell you to beg. I asked you a question." I run the tips of my fingers around her large breast and then circle her hard nipple. When she remains silent, I pinch it between my fingers and pull, making her cry out. "Answer me."

"Colt!" she cries, throwing her head back.

I drop the underwear and grab her hair, yanking her to the floor where she kneels between the coffee table and the couch, now facing my friends and Nate. I sit down on the couch behind her and wrap my free hand around her neck from behind while she starts to sob.

Lowering my mouth to her ear, I nibble on it gently. "Tell them, princess. Tell them what I said that made your pussy fucking soaked." I can feel her pulse racing, but this is part of what gets her off. I want Nate to understand what he had. He ignored her wants. Her needs. I want him to see just how beautiful she is. Even if I won't let him have her ever again, I still want him to want

116

her.

"You said..." She sniffs, pausing. "That... You said that you'll put a collar around my neck." She tries to bow her head, but I keep it up with my hand on her throat. "And lead me around the party by a leash." Her voice trembles just like her body, and I have to bite my lip to keep from smiling because I know she's soaked right now by the way she keeps rubbing her thighs together. "Naked, on all fours, with my face covered in your spit, and your cum dripping out of my cunt."

I look up to see Alex shift from side to side, adjusting himself. He's obviously enjoying the show. Finn's eyes are on her breasts, and he's practically drooling. Jenks is nodding to himself while he licks his lips. And Nate? He looks absolutely disgusted with her, and it pisses me off. It makes me want to push her even more.

I hate that she ever even dated this piece of shit. No wonder she let me fuck her in the shower. I could have been fucking her the entire time they were together. She should be thanking me. I did her a favor by making sure he saw that video of her on her knees sucking my dick.

I give her neck a little squeeze and ask, "You're not afraid of people seeing that you're my dirty little slut, are you?"

She shakes her head, softly crying. I allow the silent answer.

"Then what did I say?"

"Colt..." she cries.

"Go on, princess. I want them to hear all of it."

Knowing that I'm not going to give up on this, she swallows and then speaks softly. "That I'll be unsatisfied ... because you want them to watch me beg for you to get me off. To see me ... cry." Another sniff. "And see how desperate I am for a release."

I've taught her body to want me. To need me. I could feel it in the way she held my hand when I pulled her through the house and out the back door. "And I bet you were disappointed when I pulled you through the living room and didn't do just that."

"Ye-yes."

Letting go of her neck, I pick up the underwear, making sure everyone understands. "Telling you how I was going to humiliate and degrade you got you so wet. What does a slut do when she makes a mess?"

"She cleans it up," she whispers.

"Then do it," I order, placing them closer to her face.

She runs her tongue along the inside, licking her thong like a cat would lap up milk, her pretty, crystal-blue eyes on mine, and I feel my cock twitch inside of my pants.

"Good girl." Pulling away, she closes her eyes, and I stand from my spot on the couch. I walk over to the coffee table, pick up the drink Finn made, and shove her underwear into the glass. Using my fingers, I drown it in the scotch.

Then I put it back down and push the coffee table over to the side so the guys have a clear view of the show I'm about to give them.

RAYLEE

I'M SHAKING UNCONTROLLABLY while staring at the floor in front of me. I can't make eye contact with anyone in the room after what he made me confess. I wish he'd blindfold me, but he knows I like the humiliation.

My wrists are tied behind my back, and I'm kneeling with my legs tucked under my ass, but I can feel the wetness between them, making my thighs slippery.

It turned me on so much to admit that. The fact that Nate was present made it even better. I've told him a million times during the five weeks of our relationship what I liked, and he always dismissed it. Like I didn't know my own body. I hate it for other women like me. So many go unsatisfied because they're too afraid to tell their partner what they like and worry about being judged. I've never been a shy person, so I was able to be up front with him, but it still left me feeling empty when he rejected my needs.

Colt has never made me feel that way. And I think that's why I hate him so much. If he had turned me down, then I could have walked away from him years ago. We wouldn't have ever gotten this far. But no matter what happens, I find myself crawling back on bruised knees to beg him for more. And he's more than willing to give it to me.

Colt comes to stand on my right. "On your back. Knees up and spread your legs so I can see your cunt." he commands.

I feel my throat closing up and my clit swell at the sound of his voice. Trying to calm my breathing, I take a second before lowering my back to the floor. I position myself to where Nate and the guys have a side view of me. Biting my inner cheek, I try not to make a sound while adjusting my restrained hands underneath me. Colt crossed my wrists before he tied them, and now they're going to be digging into my back. I place my heels on the floor and spread my legs wide for him to see.

Colt kneels, running his fingers along the inside of my thigh. "Look at my slut." There's amusement in his voice, and his friends laugh. "She's so fucking wet it's running down her legs."

I whimper, arching my back, trying to relieve the pressure on my arms. It's not going to do any good. Colt always has a plan, and he had me lie like this on purpose.

He slides two fingers into me, and I buck my hips, wanting more.

"Look, princess."

I lift my head as he removes them and holds his hand up to show me his glistening fingers. He reaches out, and I open my mouth, expecting him to make me clean them, but instead, he slaps me across the face, smearing my wetness on my cheek.

I cry out at the sting and close my eyes tightly so I don't have to face his friends and my ex.

Then his hand goes back between my parted legs, and he runs his fingers over me, roughly rubbing my pussy while his thumb massages my clit.

"Fuck," I moan. "Colt ... please—"

Then he slaps it, making my back bow off the floor with a cry at the pain and pleasure it caused. Instant heat rushes to the area and makes my breath catch and my legs tighten.

"Keep them open," he growls, slapping it again—a little harder this time—and my breath is taken away.

"Colt." I choke out his name while that burning sensation between my legs intensifies. My nipples are hard, and my skin feels like it's on fire. It hurts so good.

"Did you tell Nate what happened after I took that video of you on your knees?" Colt asks.

I shake my head, sniffling.

"Why not, princess? It was so hot. Watching my best friends fuck you while I held you down and refused to let you come." He slaps my pussy again.

My swollen clit pulses. "Please," I cry, tears running down the side of my face, and I'm having trouble catching my breath. But my hips lift on their own, begging for more.

"I want it red, princess. As red as the lipstick on your perfect lips."

Whack.

I rock from side to side while arching my back, crying, and forcing my shaking legs to stay open for him. I feel wetness running down my ass to the floor.

I jump when I feel his fingers run over my pussy, and my heart races, anticipating another slap. But instead, he starts gently rubbing them back and forth, and I moan at the touch.

"That's better."

Then he's sliding his dick into me. Stretching my burning cunt for his large size. I'm thrashing under his weight, trying to stop the tears from flowing while he starts pounding into me. Not giving me any time to recover.

"Look at them." He grips my chin and forces my head to the left to face his friends and Nate. I'm having a hard time seeing them through the tears. "Look how hard they are. They enjoy watching you get off on me treating you like a slut, princess."

I whimper, blinking, and the fresh tears run down my face while my eyes can't help but fall to their jeans, and he's right. I can see how hard they all are. Even Nate.

Colt lowers his face to mine and licks my cheek where he had slapped me earlier, and then whispers in my ear, "You're so fucking beautiful." Sinking his teeth into my neck is all it takes. After the stimulation from the slaps he gave me and how hard he's now fucking me, I tumble over the edge. I'm screaming and sobbing at the same time as I come undone underneath him.

Nine

COLTON

SHE LIES BELOW me in a trance of some sort while her body shakes uncontrollably. I feel my balls tighten and pull out just in time to come all over her stomach, chest, and face. I want her covered in it.

I've lowered myself to a dog pissing on my territory. As if what I did to her hasn't already proven it. I want to make sure Nate is very clear that she's mine and will never have a chance with her again.

I lean over her and run my hands through my cum, smearing it all over her breasts and then up to her neck. Holding it in my grasp, I bend down and kiss her. She tastes like pineapple and Malibu Rum. If a sunset had a taste, this would be it. Sweet and fucking intoxicating. She moans into my mouth, her body rising up to meet mine. Always needy.

When I pull away, I whisper against her lips, "You have a mess to clean up."

I get to my feet and watch her pull her heavy body up off the floor. Tears silently run down her face, but she keeps her bloodshot eyes on mine like the good little slut she is.

Getting to her knees, I slide a hand into her hair. "Clean my cock, slut. Every drop."

Parting her lips, I shove my semi-hard cock into her mouth, forcing it down her throat—long and slow strokes at first—and I start to grow hard all over again. Pulling it out, I hold it in front of her. "Lick it. Show me how thankful you are to come."

Taking in a shaky breath, she licks her own lips before running her tongue up my shaft and wrapping them around the head of my dick. I push on her head, making her take all of me again. I hold her there until fresh tears spill down her face, and she's shifting on her knees.

I pull out and watch the drool run down her chin and neck to mix with my cum. "What do you say?" I ask.

Sucking in a deep breath, she answers roughly, "Thank you."

Going over to the coffee table, I pull it back to where it was originally and lay her across it, smashing her cum-covered chest down on it. "Wait right here."

I walk into the kitchen, grab what I need, and make my way back over. I ignore our audience. They're not important at the moment. But will come in handy soon.

Pushing the couch out of the way enough for me to kneel behind her, I spread her legs with mine and pour the oil all over my cock and along her ass. It drops off the side and down her legs. "Did he ever fuck your ass, princess?" *Also, a no.*

Her head hangs over the other side of the narrow coffee table, and she shakes it.

I grab a handful of her hair and pull it back, making her look up at them. "Tell them how much you love to have your ass fucked."

Her silent cries start to grow louder.

She knows exactly what I'm about to do. By now, she's catching on. I usually make her beg me to get off. Not this time. I'm going to have her begging me to stop making her come. I want Nate to know that he could never accomplish this with her. That he wasn't doing it right. Not like I do.

I'm not going to take the time to get her ready for my dick. After that orgasm she had, she's still on a high. I want to keep her there. I don't want her coming down until I'm done with her.

Running my dick along her ass, I push the head of my cock inside her, making her sob out my name. I bite my lip to keep from smiling at the sound.

Pulling out, I work it into her again while she squirms under me. The cum on the glass table makes her body slip around easily.

"Good girl." I kiss her shoulder while pulling back and slowly pushing inside her, listening to her soft cries, this time forcing her to take more. "Take all of me."

I smash her restrained arms between my chest and her back, pinning her down to the coffee table while I slowly spread her ass with my cock. After several thrusts, I'm balls deep inside her. I wrap my right arm around her neck, forcing her head back, and I feel her swallow against it. "Get ready, princess," I whisper in her ear.

She sucks in a deep breath, and I look up at Nate for the first time since all of this started, and his eyes are already on mine. With a look that could only be jealousy. Good, he understands what I've got.

"This is how she likes it," I tell him, and he growls behind the tape that's wrapped around his mouth and head. "This is how she comes the hardest. My cock in her ass and my arm around her throat."

I tighten my arm like a snake around its prey, slowly cutting off her air, while my hips pick up their pace, making the coffee table move across the floor with the action. She no longer fights me.

She likes being held down and fucked. But her ass? It's her weakness. It's the one thing that doesn't take much work. Then you take her air away? Goddamn, she's coming within seconds.

I kiss the side of her face, licking at the sweat, tears, smeared makeup, and bodily fluids as if it's my favorite drink in the world. Which it is.

Her body softens underneath me from lack of oxygen, and I slam my cock into her ass. The sound of my body slapping hers fills the room, and I feel her body stiffen. I smile against her cheek. "That's it. Fucking come again for me, princess. Show them just how much you love this."

Her body jerks against mine, and I loosen my hold on her neck. She's gasping for air while coughing. Her body trembles like an earthquake while she tries to beg me to stop. Just like I wanted. But I don't stop. It's my turn.

Sitting up, I grab her hips and pound into her ass, watching my cock go in and out while she lies over the coffee table completely spent. She wouldn't be able to crawl right now if I told her to. The view of her tight ass swallowing my cock has my breath quickening and balls tightening.

I push inside her, a growl releasing from deep in my chest as I come, filling her ass. When I pull out, I smile down at her red, swollen pussy from my hand slapping it.

I give myself a few seconds to catch my breath before I stand and reach my hand out to Finn. "Give me your knife."

He hands it over, and I cut the zip tie binding her wrists. Lifting her up off the table, I sit down on the couch with her shaking body in my lap, and I look at the guys. "What do you say, princess? They should get to come too, don't you think?"

She doesn't answer me. Instead, her head falls back off my arm and her eyes slowly close. I've worn her out.

I look up at the guys and smile. "Go ahead. Play with him."

Nate jumps up from his seat, but Alex grabs his hair, keeping him in place. Finn rips his shirt down the middle and tears it off before tossing it to the side. Then Jenks grabs him, pushing him onto the coffee table on his back. His arms secured underneath him. They're like fucking animals.

He tries to fight them, but three against one are shitty odds. They each undo their jeans and pull their hard dicks out. Finn shoves his knee into Nate's neck to hold him down while Alex straddles him, making sure not to put too much weight on the table and break it.

I smile. His back is covered in my cum, and soon, his front will be covered in theirs. Standing from the couch, I carry her over to the kitchen table with one last idea. Then I'm leaving with her. Taking her home and putting her in my bed where she will wake up in the morning.

"Colt?" she says in a hoarse voice.

"Yeah, princess?"

"I want to go home." She yawns, her eyes still closed.

"Soon," I tell her. "Just one more thing."

"I can't—come again, Colt. Please ..."

I smile at her words and come up to the kitchen table. I set her on her feet at the corner. "Lean over the table," I say, gently kissing her cheek.

She gladly lays her stomach onto it, resting her body. I remove my belt from my jeans that I still wear and bend down, wrapping it around the corner leg of the table and her thighs, securing them to it. Then standing, I walk over to the fridge and open the freezer to see a frosted mug in it. I pull it out and pour some ice in it along with some bourbon. Then I look up to see her passed out on the table, arms fanned out above her head. I hear grunts and a slew of curse words, and look up to see my friends each coming all over Nate.

"Bring him in here," I call out before taking a drink.

They yank him up from the coffee table and drag his ass into the kitchen, where they sit him in a chair. I walk over to him and smile at the look of fucking hatred in his eyes. *Fucking bastard.* I place my hands on the table and lean over into his cum-covered face. "This is what happens when you touch something that isn't yours."

He throws his weight around in the chair but doesn't go anywhere with Jenks's hand in his hair.

"I didn't train her to be the good little slut she is for someone else to use."

His eyes widen at that.

"Did you think that video was our first time?" My friends laugh. "We've been fucking for five years, Nate." I tap the side of his face a few times. "I did you a favor by making sure you saw that video. Gave you a reason to stay the fuck away. That obviously didn't work. Maybe tonight helped make you understand just how serious I am. But just in case you forget again, I'll give you one more."

I place the frozen mug on Raylee's ass cheek, and a soft whimpering sound comes from her parted lips, but her eyes stay closed. "Hold that there, please," I ask Alex, and he takes over for me.

Holding out my hand, I look at Finn. "I need your wallet."

He pulls it out of his back pocket and hands it to me.

Then I add, "Find something to tie her down with." Because I can't have her fight me with what I'm about to do.

RAYLEE

"HERE, USE THIS." I hear someone say, maybe Alex? I don't know. I can't hear much over the blood rushing in my ears. The room is spinning, my head pounds, and my entire body aches. I can't come again. My body won't be able to take it. I, at least, need to use the restroom, take a bath, and get a nap. Not in that order. But any one of those would be good right now.

My lips are numb from all the alcohol, and I can't feel my feet either. My body won't stop shaking. It's out of my control at this point.

Lifting the side of my face up off the table, I look up through heavy eyes to see Jenks and Alex standing in front of me.

Alex has rope in his hands. Jenks grabs my wrists and pulls them out as far as they'll go in front of me. Crossing my wrists, Alex takes the rope and ties it around my wrists several times, and then pulls it even tighter, making me whimper as he stretches me across the kitchen table. He kneels and secures the other end of the rope to one of the legs.

I'm stretched as far as I can go, diagonal across it. No give at all. "What are you doing?" I ask, trying to yank on them, but I get nowhere. It's too tight, and I'm too weak.

Tilting my head to the other side, I look around to see what is happening. I meet a set of brown eyes, and they are glaring at me. Nate is seated in a chair. He's shirtless and—looks like cum is all over his body. But that can't be right. I'm seeing things. Or hallucinating. It can happen when being choked out while fucking. I swear, I've seen the tunnel of light that everyone talks about before you die when Colt was fucking me one time. It was a high I've never been able to reach since. But I'm close to it tonight.

I try to look over my shoulder for him, but I just don't have the strength, so I lay my head back down and close my eyes as something cold touches my ass, making me hiss in a breath.

What the hell is he doing?

"Jenks, grab her underwear. It's in the glass on the coffee table." Colt's voice sounds far away.

My eyes flutter open seconds later when I feel my thong being shoved into my mouth, and Jenks is right in my face. "Bite down on that," he tells me.

I do what he says, and I taste the scotch invading my mouth from the material. I swallow some, the rest runs out and onto the table. Something cold is on my ass cheek, making me shiver, but is quickly replaced with a hand, and I flinch. "I haven't even gotten started." I hear Colt say before slapping it. "Did you feel that?'

"Yeah," I mumble through the gag. *Why wouldn't I be able to?*

"Sorry, princess, but this is going to hurt," he tells me, then I feel a burning sensation on my ass. Like something is ripping through it.

I slam my head into the table, biting down on the material to keep from screaming at the top of my lungs. My breath momentarily taken away by the sheer pain. My entire body tenses up, and I pull on the restraints that have me tied down to the table.

Ten

COLTON

I STAND AND look over her ass as blood runs down her leg from the four letters I just carved into her. Bringing the razor blade to my mouth, I can't help but run my tongue across it, licking up her blood before tossing it onto the table. Then I lean down and run my tongue along her ass, licking it clean too. "Beautiful," I whisper.

Gripping a handful of her hair, I gently pull her face up off the table and rip the thong from her mouth. Then wrap my other hand around her jaw, tilting her head so she's looking over her shoulder at me. I slam my lips to hers, letting her taste her own blood on my tongue along with her tears that run down her face.

She doesn't kiss me back with as much enthusiasm as I have, but I expected that. "Good girl, princess. Good girl," I praise, trying to calm her down.

Her bloodshot eyes meet mine. "Please?" she begs.

"I know. We're going home."

She closes her eyes, and her shoulders shake as a silent sob wracks her body. Letting go of her, I walk to the sink and take a hand towel, running warm water over it. I then walk back over to her and gently press it to the wound, trying to stop the bleeding.

Jenks runs down the stairs with some ointment in one hand and a large bandage in the other. "Here you go." He hands them over to me.

Removing the towel, I unscrew the lid on the ointment and squeeze some onto my finger, and then rub it on the letters of my name.

She quietly sobs while flinching.

"Almost done," I tell her. Opening up the bandage, I place it on her ass. Then I bend down and undo my belt from around her legs while Alex unties her wrists.

"Jenks, go bring her car around," I say, and he takes off out the door. I don't want to have to carry her through the party like this. Ripping my shirt up and over my head, I place it on her and then pick her up in my arms. She buries her face into my bare chest.

"What do you want to do with him?" Finn asks, pointing at Nate, who sits in the kitchen chair, mouth duct-taped, and wrists tied behind his back, covered in our cum.

I laugh. "Tie him to the chair and leave him. Someone will find him. Eventually."

Just then, the door opens, and Jenks enters once again. "It's right outside."

"See you guys back at home." I walk her outside and place her in the passenger seat of her car and buckle her seat belt.

"Please?" she says in a soft voice.

I push her wild hair from her wet face and cup her cheek. "We're going home, princess."

She doesn't even bother to open her heavy eyes. She just nods once, and her head falls to the side. I'm losing her fast. She had been drinking, then add what I just did to her for the past hour, and she's exhausted.

Shutting her door, I get in the driver's seat and take her home.

RAYLEE

I WAKE TO a dark room, moaning at the pain I feel in my entire body. I've never been beaten with a baseball bat before, but I imagine this is what it feels like.

A hand wraps around my waist, pulling my back into a hard body, and I freeze. My eyes dart around the room, trying to remember what all happened last night. Went to Mike's party, but it was really Mitch's. Nate was there. Tried to force me to leave with him. Then Colt… Fuck, that's where things go black, and I shove the man off me and jump out of bed.

My shaking legs manage to get me over to the door where I know the light switch is, and I flip it on. My worst nightmare is coming true. "What the fuck, Colt?" I bark out when I see him lying in his bed.

He stretches and sits up, the covers falling to his lap, showing me his smooth chest. His eyes meet mine, and he smirks. "What are you doing? Come back to bed." He pats the side next to him. "I'm hungry." His eyes drop to my legs, and I realize I'm naked.

"What in the fuck are you doing?" I ask again, confused as hell. I never stay the night in his bed. Ever. Not once. We fuck, and then go our separate ways.

"Turn off the light and come back to bed," he orders, lying down and rolling onto his stomach. The covers shift, showing me a perfect view of his ass.

I think about doing what he says for a second, but that morning in the kitchen reminds me that the guys said they always eat pussy when they wake up with a woman in their bed. I shake my head, refusing to allow that this morning. He has some explaining to do.

Leaning against the dresser behind me, I hiss in a breath when it feels like something just stabbed me. "What…?" I turn around to see what it is, but there's nothing on the dresser, so I run my hand over my butt. "Fuck." I hiss at the feel again. *What the hell is on my ass?*

I look over my shoulder, staring at my backside in the mirror, and see a bandage. *What the fuck?* A scream erupts from my lips when I rip it off, making him jump up from his bed.

"What's wrong?" Colt asks, walking over to me.

I throw my hands up, and he stops. "Please, tell me this is a joke?" I ask, tears stinging my eyes.

"What are you talking about?" He feigns innocence.

I fist my hands. "Why is your name carved into my ass?" I growl.

A smirk spreads across his face. "I didn't see you stopping me last night."

"I can't even remember last night," I yell at him. "Why would you do that?"

"Because Nate needed the reminder that you belong to me," he replies simply. As if carving his name into my ass is totally acceptable.

"No, no, no." I place my shaking hands in my already tangled hair. "You've got to be kidding me."

He reaches out, grabbing my arm, and yanks me to his naked body. "It's no big deal."

I reach up and slap him across the face. "This ... this is a very big deal." *He branded me.* Made me his in a way I never thought possible. "What if I carved my name into you?" I snap.

He turns, walking over to his nightstand and opens up the top drawer. Removing his pocketknife, he slaps it open. Coming back over to me, he holds it out to me, handle first.

I just stare at it. It's one that I got him for his birthday five years ago. I told him to *go bleed to death.* I got it for him after he got me a dildo that said *go fuck yourself.*

"Do it," he says, offering me the knife.

"Colt," I whisper his name. Either he's lost his fucking mind or this is a game. This is where things have gone, and I'm not sure what to do.

With his free hand, he raises my chin to look up at him. "Do it, princess. You don't even have to tie me down. I'd gladly lie there while I bleed for you."

My breath hitches at his words. How can he make me hate him and want it at the same time? Why do I always feel like I'm losing this game? I swear, if he wanted to, he could drive me insane in a matter of days. It wouldn't take much at this point.

"Straddle my hips and carve your name into my chest, princess. Let the world see how much you love me."

My eyes search his, trying to find an ounce of deceit. He's trying to manipulate me and make me look stupid. "I don't love you," I whisper.

Dear Lord, what all happened last night? What did I say? Just a few nights ago, we were in my shower expressing how much we hate one another while fucking. Now he's dropping the word love?

"No?" he asks, frowning. "I think you do, Raylee."

I swallow at the use of my real name. It's always princess to him. Shaking my head, I take a step back, and my ass hits the damn dresser again, making me whimper. But he's already stepped closer, pinning me in place.

"Have you ever wondered why we can't let each other go?" He lowers his face to my neck and gently kisses my racing pulse. "Why you so willingly crawl back to me after every failed relationship you've ever had? Or why you beg me to fuck you? It's because you know that no one will ever satisfy you like I do."

"Love and sex aren't the same thing," I breathe, trying to think of a reasonable argument.

"Oh, they are, princess." He pulls back and lifts the knife in front of my face, making me suck in a shaky breath. "No other man will love you the way I do." He runs the tip of the blade down my chest bone, and I hold my breath. "No other man will bring you to your knees like I do." The knife trails down over my stomach and my pelvic bone. I spread my legs when he shows no sign of stopping. "Or make you crawl like I do." The tip falls between my legs.

"Colt?" I swallow nervously, and whisper, "What are you doing?"

He brings it to a stop, the blade sitting between my legs, the cold metal making my nipples hard. His eyes meet mine when he says, "You're my dirty little slut, princess. Mine. And that's why I carved my name into your ass. So you'll always have a reminder that I own you." A tear runs down my face, and he watches it with amusement.

"No." I shake my head once, denying what he just said. It can't be true.

He laughs softly, and his eyes drop to my legs. "Look what I did to you last night. You were such a needy slut. Starving for whatever I would give you."

My stomach knots at his words because I can't remember what all I did for him, but I'm sure he's right. He's my weakness.

"Begged me in front of your ex to get you off. Then to stop making you come. Admitting to my friends fucking you. And how much you love it when I humiliate you."

I whimper as fresh tears fill my eyes, making his face nothing but a blurry figure.

"They were all so fucking hard for you, princess. I had to show them that they could never have you again." Stepping back, he removes the blade from between my legs, and I let out a shaky breath. Bringing it to his lips, he licks the flat edge of the blade that was pressed up against my pussy, and my legs threaten to buckle. "Here." He holds it out to me. "Make me yours."

Make him mine? Colton Knox will never be mine. He'll never belong to anyone. Men like him don't settle down, especially with a woman like me. I'm a toy. Something fun to play with. And I've been fine with that. So why pretend now? Why make me think there's a possibility of anything more?

I've never wanted more. Not with him. I hate him.

But do I really? Can you be physically attracted to someone you hate? Why do I allow him to put me in positions where I know he'll humiliate me? Why did I willingly move in with him? Why do I let him control my life?

It can't be love. It has to be convenience. I've been using him. Not the other way around. I've told myself over and over that a woman can treat a man the same way they treat women. He's been my toy. And when I'm done with him, I'll walk away.

"No." The single word trembles on my lips, exposing my lack of confidence in my answer.

And just when I think I can't be any more confused. A smile spreads across his face—one of those *I fucking hate you* smiles. I've seen it too often over the past six years. His green eyes light up like a Christmas tree.

My body is shaking, rage coming over me, when he reaches up and pushes some loose hair behind my ear ever so gently. Stepping into me, he tilts his head to the side. "I told you that video was nothing compared to what I'd do to you for setting my car on fire."

Eleven

COLTON

I FUCKING LOVE this bitch! I've got to be the dumbest man in the world. I thought things would go differently this morning. I wasn't lying when I told her to carve her name into my chest, but I saw the look on her face. She doesn't feel the same way about me. She thought I was playing a game.

Fuck, maybe I am. I don't know what the fuck is going on. Too many lines have been crossed that nothing makes sense anymore.

Like right now, she's standing in front of me, silently crying, and all I can think about is throwing her to the floor and holding this knife to her throat while I fuck her wet cunt, and she begs for her life. Something to give me control over the situation again because I've lost her.

Whatever hold I had on her is gone. I went too far last night. Or maybe she went too far with letting me have my way.

I step back, close the pocketknife, and point at my door. "Get the fuck out of my room."

She doesn't need to be told twice. Ripping my door open, she runs out, and I slam it shut behind her.

"Fuck!" I throw the knife across my room. She rejected me. She gave Nate five weeks of her life, but won't even give me a fucking chance?

I brought her home last night, gave her a bath, and put her in my bed. Granted, she was in and out of consciousness for most of it. But I took care of her. It was the gentlest I've ever been with her, and she doesn't even remember it. She clung to me. Needed me. It made me feel like a man. A protector. I've always used her, but this was different. I was finally something she needed other than a fuck. Or so I thought. I was obviously wrong.

My cell ringing on the nightstand gets my attention. I walk over to it and hit answer when I see it's Mitch. "What?" I bark out.

"Hey, man." He sighs. "I just wanted to give you a heads-up on Nate."

"What about him?" I demand, pulling a pair of boxers on.

"I forgot that I told you guys that you could use the in-law suite last night. Anyway, I found him earlier this morning, and he was livid."

"Good."

"I just wanted to warn you. He was talking some mad shit. That he was going to fuck you up—"

I snort. "Thanks for the warning." Nate doesn't want to even come near me. I'll break his fucking face next time I see him.

"I'm serious, Colt. After I untied him and removed the duct tape from around his mouth, he was throwing shit around. Running his mouth about begging … I don't know what he was talking about, and he wouldn't explain it to me, but he promised I'd understand soon enough."

Well, at least he thinks I got the girl. I'd rather him not know that she turned me down. No matter what happens between Raylee and me, I know she'll never go back to him. "Thanks." I hang up before he can say anything else.

A knock comes at my door, and I open it up, expecting it to be her but let out a growl when I see it's Finn. "What do you want?" I should have stayed in bed.

"Everything okay?" he asks, stepping into my room.

"Yep," I lie. "Why wouldn't it be?"

"Because I just saw Raylee run out of the house with a bag packed and tears rolling down her face. She was obviously upset."

I run a hand through my hair.

"I don't want to get involved," he adds.

"Then don't," I snap at him.

He closes my door, letting me know that's exactly what he's about to do. "Don't get me wrong, last night was fun—fucking

140

great—but the show you put on was equivalent to the one where she burned your car down."

"Your point?" I growl, not liking where this is headed.

"My point is, what the fuck are you doing, man?" He points at my door. "You two are going to kill each other trying to prove that you don't love one another."

I snort. "We don't—"

"She may not love you, but you're in love with her."

His words are like a punch to my gut. I never considered her not feeling the same way about me. She comes crawling back to me every time I push her away. I guess, over time, I thought I could make her love me the same way I make her want me.

I sit down on the edge of my bed, and admit, "We got into a fight."

"And?"

"And what?" I snap. Before he can answer, I add, "She'll get over it and return home. Or come back to set it on fire." Either way, she'll return. She always does.

"Ahh, I see." He sits down beside me. "Can I say something without you punching me?"

I give a rough laugh. "No promises."

"You've been hell-bent on making her as miserable as you for the past six years. Now is the time to fight for her as hard as you've fought the feelings you have for her."

I look over at him, and he pulls a joint out from behind his ear, staring down at it. "She's got one more year left of college, and then she's gone, Colt."

"She won't ..." I trail off as his words sink in.

I've done whatever I needed to do to keep her in my life. To make sure she stays close to me. Afraid if she put too much distance between us that I wouldn't be able to pull her back to me. What will I do to keep her here with me after graduation? What if she moves across the country? The thought alone is crippling.

"What?" He laughs. "She won't leave? She will. Why would she stay here in a house with four guys?" Pulling his lighter out of his pocket, he puts the joint to his lips and lights it up. Taking a hit, he tilts his head back and blows it out slowly. "No matter how much she enjoys being your slut, she'll eventually want to be someone's wife." He slaps my shoulder and holds out the joint. "It's human nature. A woman wants to be more than a booty call,

Colt. And after all the shit you've put her through, I think Raylee has earned the right to be happy. Whether that's with you or someone else."

Both of our cell phones go off at the same time, signaling a text message. I don't even bother to look at mine because he removes his from his pocket. "It's Tyson. He wants us at Blackout in thirty."

I hand him back the joint, not in the mood to get high. I'd much rather go and beat some guy's face in.

RAYLEE

I'M DRIVING DOWN the road, my hands fisting the steering wheel. I've got all of my weight on my left ass cheek because my right one stings from where he branded me. Fuck him and whatever games he thinks he can play.

I ran back to my room, used the restroom, then threw on a pair of shorts and a T-shirt. Didn't even bother with a damn bra and tossed some shit into a bag. I'll go spend a few nights at my mom and Cliff's. I hate that Colt will think he won by running me off, but I need some fresh air.

Need time to regroup and figure out my next step.

I thought about calling Tatum to see what she's doing, but her cell is in the back seat of my car along with mine. She had left with Billy last night and forgot about it. I then thought I'd call and check on Raven, but when I tried to turn mine on, I got nothing. The motherfucker must have died. I didn't have much battery left anyway.

Looking up in my rearview mirror, I see a truck on my ass. Instead of brake-checking them, I speed up. So do they.

"What the fuck?" I growl, not in the mood for some asshole and their road rage today.

Whoever it is, punches on the gas and speeds around me. They swerve over in front of me, forcing me to slam on the brake. "Fuck!" I hiss as everything in the passenger seat falls to the floorboard. I lay on the horn, and they speed off once again, taking a corner too fast.

I let off the brake and accelerate, going slower than I was as I get my breathing back to normal and rack my brain for anything that happened last night. I'm still drawing a blank. How do I not remember? There's no way I told him I love him, right? Like that's not even a word in my vocabulary, let alone something I would say to Colt.

I'm not one of those dumb girls who confuses sex with love. I don't need to cuddle afterward. I don't need a daily text, or a phone call. You can fuck me and go on your way, and I'm okay with that. So why do I feel like what he said had some kind of truth to it? Why is Colt the drug that I can't seem to quit? Out of every relationship that I've failed, he's the one guy I always go back to. I can dump a guy and not even think of him again. But Colt? I think about him all the time. Even when I'm with other guys.

Shifting in my leather seat, I hiss in a breath at the sting on my ass cheek. "You're so dead." I growl through gritted teeth. I will set his ass on fire this time.

"Think, Ray." I slam my palm on the steering wheel. What the fuck happened? How did I even get home …

I open my heavy eyes, blinking a few times. I ache everywhere. I bring my shaking hands to my face, and they're wet. "What …?" I clear my throat, my voice scratchy, and it hurts to swallow, making me flinch.

"You're okay." I hear that familiar voice in my ear from behind me.

I don't even have the energy to turn around and look at him. Instead, I sink into what I realize is his bathtub, my back against his chest, and I close my eyes, enjoying the hot water burning my sensitive skin.

"You did so good tonight, princess," he whispers in my ear. His lips trail down to kiss my neck, and my head falls to the side, silently begging him to kiss me there. "Fuck, you're so perfect. Tell me again that you're mine."

"I'm yours." I lick my numb lips. "I'm yours, Colt," I repeat. "I've always been yours." Isn't that what this is about? He's my addiction. My drug. I'll never get enough of him. He knows it, and I know it. I've spent so much time on my knees for him that I don't even care if I ever walk again.

"Goddamn right, beautiful." He smiles against my neck. He removes his lips from my wet skin and replaces them with his hand. Giving me a little squeeze, he adds, "You're mine now and forever."

"Forever," I agree.

No. Tears run down my face as that memory gets through the fog that was last night. It's not true. I don't believe it. My heart hammers in my chest, and I sniff. I haven't fallen in love with him. It's not supposed to happen this way. Not with him.

"You did so good tonight, princess." He said that to me. What did I do? Did I beg him to love me?

Taking the corner, I see the truck again, but I'm too slow. They slam on their brakes, and I don't have enough time to stop, so I rear-end them.

My entire body stiffens, knowing it's coming as my seat belt tightens on my chest. My body goes forward at the impact while the airbag blows up in my face. I breathe in a cloud of dust, trying to get my vision to return. Everything is blurry, my ears ring, and my skin burns.

I hear the sound of metal being pried open and a hand grips my hair. I'm being yanked out, but my seat belt keeps me in the car.

"Fuck." Someone hisses. Then they're reaching across me and undoing it.

My head falls forward, and I feel something warm running down my face. "What ...?"

"Shut the fuck up." I'm yanked from my car, and I fall to my knees on the asphalt, unable to stand.

I catch sight of my shaking hands, and they've got cuts on them.

A hand grips my hair, pulling me to my feet, and I'm dragged away from my car and into a new one. My heavy eyes close while I try to breathe. My chest is tight, and I feel like something is sitting on it.

Twelve

NATE

I TOSS HER into the driver's side of the truck that I borrowed from a friend. I didn't want her to see me coming.

She falls across the center console, and I shove her over as I hop inside and slam my door. "I—" She coughs, her bleach-blond hair sticking to her now bloody face. "Need a hospital."

I ram my elbow into her face, slamming her head back and knocking her out. Her body slides down the seat a little, and I don't even bother putting a seat belt on her. I'm going to do worse things to her than a car wreck could.

Throwing the truck in drive, I step on the gas and pull back onto the road.

I never meant to hurt her. Not like this. But this isn't about her. It's about Colt and his friends. They humiliated me by forcing me to watch her beg him for sex. To get off.

I was disgusted with myself that it made me hard.

She told me what she liked, and I was repulsed by it. Told her it wasn't for me. Then when I watched Colt show me exactly what she had been explaining to me, I fucking enjoyed it.

Pulling into Mike and Mitch's parents' house, I drive around the back to the in-law suite. I was told last night that Mike is in jail. I can't take her to my house because my roommate will find out what I'm doing. He's at work, but his girlfriend has practically moved in with us. She's always fucking there. Plus, I'd much rather take her to the place where they humiliated me. A dose of her own medicine sort of thing.

Bringing the truck to a stop, I get out and walk over to the passenger's door and yank her out of it. I throw her over my shoulder and walk her inside.

Laying her on the couch, I make my way over to the kitchen table and grab a few things that I'm going to need.

Colt might have humiliated me, but he has no clue that I've got his slut right now. And he won't know until I want him to. By then, it'll be too late. I've always considered myself a nice guy, but if she wants to be a whore, then I'll treat her like one.

I roll her onto her stomach and pull her arms behind her back, taking the roll of duct tape and wrapping it around her wrists several times before ripping it off. Then I shove her onto her back again. A moan escapes her busted lips, but her eyes remain closed.

I tear off her T-shirt and am not surprised to find her braless. Looking over her chest, I see a bruise already from where the seat belt stopped her from hitting the steering wheel. That's going to hurt. Smiling, I shred the material and throw all but one piece to the floor.

I tie a knot in it and then shove it into her mouth, bringing it around the back of her head and tying it off to gag her. I don't need to hear her beg. I heard enough of that shit last night.

It was pathetic. The way she willingly did whatever he told her to like she was a trained pet.

I didn't train her to be the good little slut she is for someone else to use. That is what Colt had told me. Five fucking years they've been hooking up. How did I not see it? How did no one know this? Well, obviously his friends did. Maybe that's why he allowed them to fuck her too. To keep their secret.

I wonder how he'll feel when he realizes I used her too. Satisfied with what I've done so far, I fall down onto the chair they tied me in last night and prop my feet up on the coffee table, waiting.

I want to make sure she's awake for what I'm going to do to her. Just because I don't want to hear her beg doesn't mean I don't want to see her cry.

The front door opens and in walks Mike. He comes to an abrupt stop when he sees me. "What the fuck are you doing here, Nate?"

Sabotage

RAYLEE

My heavy eyes flutter open and immediately close. I feel like I'm spinning. The world tilting. I can taste blood, and my tongue is swollen. My head pounds worse than when I woke up in Colt's bed this morning.

What happened?

Why does everything hurt? My body feels … sluggish.

I open my eyes again to see a white ceiling. It looks familiar. Where am I?

"What are you doing here? You're supposed to be in jail." I hear a voice far off.

"I got released a few hours ago."

"I need to borrow your place for a day or two."

"Okay," the man says slowly. "You can stay as long as you need to."

"Thanks, man."

I look around, my eyes starting to focus better. My body is regaining feeling, and I realize that my arms are underneath me. And it feels like some kind of tape is wrapped around my wrists. My breathing picks up, causing my chest to hurt, and that's when I feel something in my mouth.

I immediately close my eyes, pretending to be asleep while taking inventory of my body. To what all I can use. What I can feel.

"What the fuck?" I hear the second man bark, and I realize it's Mike's voice. "What in the fuck are you doing, Nate?"

Fuck? Why am I with Nate?

Mike goes on. "What is Raylee doing in my fucking house?"

"Calm down." He chuckles. I lie still, trying to come up with a plan, not wanting to interrupt their conversation. The more I know, the better my odds are of getting the fuck out of here. "No one knows she's here."

My stomach knots at that. I had run out of Colt's house. Then I hit the truck. It was a setup. Nate must have been watching me. My cell was dead in my car. I have no means to reach the outside world.

"What the fuck, man?" Mike hisses. "She has to go. She can't be here."

"No one will think to look for her here."

"I know she's here," Mike argues.

"They humiliated me, Mike." Nate growls. "Colt, Alex, Finn, and Jenks. They fucking tied me up, then held me down and jerked off all over me last night."

"Some people pay good money for that kind of shit."

"Mike!" he snaps. "This is not a joke."

"What are you going to do, fuck her?" Mike snorts.

"You did. You took her virginity."

"I had no clue she was a virgin. Once I realized that she was, I was out. Colt beat my ass the next time he saw me at practice for that shit. Coach had to bribe the principal from suspending us both."

"So you're saying you're afraid of him?" Nate scoffs.

"No, I'm saying she's not worth it. She's his fucking whore, Nate. She always has been and always will be. He's ruined every relationship she's ever had. Or will have in the future. Let her go."

A hand grabs hold of my hair and yanks me off the couch to my knees. I bite into the gag to keep from making a sound. Nate yanks my head back and forces me to look up at them while he kneels behind me. I look around aimlessly, pretending to be in and out of consciousness.

"This is your chance, Mike." He reaches around and touches my breasts, and that's when I realize I'm topless.

I feel vomit rise, and I try to shake him off, but he wraps an arm around my throat from behind and takes away my air.

"You can have a piece. And when we're done with her, we'll cut her up and dump her body in the woods. Animals will eat her. She'll never be found because nothing will be left of her."

Tears blur my vision, and my chest heaves, trying to suck in a breath while he holds me in place. He's got it all planned out.

"Look." Mike glances down at his watch, unbothered that I've been kidnapped and gagged. "I have to be somewhere in fifteen minutes. If I don't show up, they'll come here. And since you're using my place as a stash house, we don't want that. I've got to go. Stay here with her, and I'll be back in an hour."

Nate lets go of me and shoves me forward, my body hitting the floor. I open my mouth as wide as it'll go to try to suck in a breath around the gag while I hack up my lungs, making my already sore chest hurt even more.

"Take your time." Nate waves him off.

"Don't touch her until I get back," Mike warns.

"So you want a piece?"

"They work for the Lords," he barks out as if that's supposed to mean something.

"The Lords are a myth. Some made-up shit," Nate argues.

"Whether you believe in them or not, Colt, Jenks, Alex, and Finn kill people. That's a fact," Mike growls.

"And you're afraid they'll come after you."

"No, Jesus Christ, Nate. I don't want you doing anything that can't be covered up. I don't need cops at my house because they found a dead body. And a blood trail that leads them back here. So sit your ass down, have a drink, and keep your hands to yourself. When I return, we'll figure out a plan. Together." Mike turns and runs out the door, slamming it behind him.

"Guess it's just you and me." A boot kicks my shoulder, shoving me onto my back, and I close my eyes, trying to calm my breathing. Maybe if he thinks I passed out, he'll leave me alone.

I feel his boot against my neck. He presses down on it, taking away my air again, and I can't fake it. Panic sinks in as the pressure gets heavier and heavier, crushing me. My eyes spring open, and I look up at him glaring down at me while I kick my legs, trying to fight for a breath.

"Well, Ray." He gives me a chilling smile. "You're not as good of a faker as you thought."

When he removes his boot, I roll onto my side and suck in a shaky breath while I cough, making my throat burn. The gag makes it even more difficult to breathe.

He grips my hair and yanks me up, dragging me up onto the couch. Then he's untying the gag from around my mouth and tosses it onto the coffee table.

"God, I never thought you were a coward," I say roughly as he walks around to go sit in a chair across from me.

He throws his head back laughing, making his Adam's apple bob. "I always knew you were a whore, Ray. Why do you think I dated you in the first place?"

"Fuck you!" I shout, my hands trying to fight the tape around my wrists. I need something to cut it with. If I could break some glass…

"Ah, Ray." He removes his phone from his pocket and punches in a password, then stands it up against a bowl on the table, facing me, and I see it's recording. "Since you like to record yourself." He stands from the chair and walks over to me.

I lift my feet, since I still have my tennis shoes on, and try to kick him away, but he shoves them down and slaps me across the face. So hard it knocks me off my sore ass and down to my side. I cry out into the couch cushion, tears stinging my eyes at the force. I like being slapped during sex, but Colt has never hit me that hard.

"Shh." He sits me back up. "It's okay." He pushes my hair from my tear-streaked and snot-covered face. I duck my head, but he grips my hair and yanks my head back before slapping me again.

I spit on him.

He wipes it from his face and smiles at me. Yanking me from the couch, he shoves me to my knees and holds me hostage in front of his phone by my hair. "Tell him," he growls in my ear. "Tell Colt that you're my dirty fucking slut now."

"No—"

He slams my face into the coffee table, and I see fucking stars. Pain explodes behind my eyes, and my vision goes black for a moment. Blood runs out of the corner of my already busted lips.

Pulling my limp head back, he reaches forward and fixes the phone that got knocked over in the process. "Tell him," he snaps. "Tell him how much you're going to enjoy me tying you down and letting my friends fuck you." He grips my busted face with his free hand. "Hmm? They're going to use you like the whore you are, baby."

Showing my bloody teeth, I look at him in the phone, "Fuck you, you piece of—"

"Fucking hardheaded bitch!" He slams me into the table again, but he lets me go and I fall to my side on the floor this time.

Coughing, I spit blood out and close my heavy eyes. My right one is swelling. I can feel my heartbeat in my cheek, pounding away.

He steps over me and goes into the kitchen area. I see the phone has fallen off the table as well but it's still recording, laying on its side in front of me.

I look like I've been stung by a bee. My upper lip is so swollen. I've got multiple cuts on my bloody face. I'm not sure if they're from the car wreck or him.

Tears sting my eyes, and I have to look away from the phone, so I don't get upset. Now is not the time. I can cry about it later when I'm alive and free from this psycho.

Looking around, I see him standing in the kitchen. His hands are on the table. There are a lot of power tools, along with tape and ropes, covering the surface. I'm sure I can use something on there to fight him off with. I just need my hands free.

Rolling more onto my chest, I move my wrists, twisting them back and forth, trying to loosen the tape. There's more give than there was when I woke up, and it gives me hope.

My adrenaline is pumping, making my breathing pick up. It's up to me. No one is coming to save me. I refuse to let Nate kill me and feed me to the animals. Who knows how long he'll drag this on? He's already proven that he's going to torture me for the hell of it. Have his fun like I'm a toy.

And Colt? He's not going to be out looking for me. He thinks I'm mad at him. Hate him. He won't send out a search party when I don't come home tonight.

"They humiliated me," Nate says to himself. "Fuck them!" Then lets out a scream, leaning over and shoving everything off the table and onto the floor. "Son of a bitch!"

I sit up, pressing my back into the front of the couch to hide my arms from his view. Not wanting him to see what I'm doing. I've only got an hour before Mike returns. He wasn't on Nate's side, but he also wasn't on mine. There's no way I can get free from both of them.

"They jerked off all over me. Those sick bastards covered me in their cum." He keeps mumbling to himself. "Fucking humiliated me because of you." His eyes lock on mine, and I freeze, praying he can't tell that I have a plan. Pushing away from the table, he walks over to me but pauses, his eyes on the floor. My throat tightens when I see what he's looking at. I try to take in a calming breath.

No. Please, God. No.

Bending down, he picks up the roll of duct tape and continues to walk the short distance over to me. "They fucking gagged me. I'll do the same to you."

I lift my chin, refusing to give him the satisfaction of my fear. "You also got turned on. What's that say about you?" I don't remember what happened, but Colt had told me that this morning. And by the way his face morphs into rage, I hit a nerve. Good. I want him irrational. I can control the situation better.

He grips the back of my neck and shoves my face into the floor while he straddles my back, cramming my restrained arms between me and his body. I grit my teeth at the pain. Gripping my hair, he picks it up off the floor and starts wrapping the tape around my entire face. I fight him with all I have, but I'm just too weak. Some gets in my mouth, and I taste my hair. He wraps it over and over until I'm afraid he's going to place it over my nose too, suffocating me. But he stops and stands up off me.

My head falls to the floor, and I suck in a breath through my nose, reminding myself to stay calm. The last thing I want to do is have a panic attack. I've never had one before, but I know if I do, it won't be good. My air is already restricted.

He grabs my ankles and pulls me across the floor back toward the kitchen, and then he's ripping my shorts and underwear off. I cry into the tape, unable to stop myself because I know what's coming.

Rolling onto my back, I kick my feet out and buck my hips, trying to harm him in any way. But he drops to his knees, straddling me, and wraps both hands around my neck, cutting off my air. Tears run down the corners of my eyes, and I fight harder. Refusing to give up and let him win.

"Beg him now!" he screams in my face, spit flying from his mouth. "Huh, you fucking whore. Beg Colt to fuck you now."

I arch my neck, trying to get my face away from his, but he starts shaking me, and dots cover my vision, and that pounding in my face intensifies. My body starts to convulse while my chest heaves, and my attempt to fight back grows weaker. My eyes grow heavy, rolling back.

He lets go, and the blood rushes to my head. I'm wheezing, face pounding, and throat burning. I blink the tears out of my eyes, trying to get my bearings back. My body is too heavy to move, which gives him enough time to unzip his pants. He readjusts himself between my legs, spreading them wide, and he spits on my pussy.

I arch my back as a sob wracks my body at how weak he's made me. I don't have any strength left right now.

"Fucking bitch," he mumbles to himself. "I'll show you all who is in charge here." When he pushes his cock into me, my body stiffens, and he slaps my face.

The force has me looking underneath the coffee table, and that damn phone is still propped up, still filming. I just stare at it as my body rocks back and forth on the floor.

"Whose slut are you now, Raylee?" he asks. "Mine."

I let my eyes fall closed. Maybe if he thinks I'm dead, he'll stop. But I'm not giving up yet. No. I just need a few more seconds to recover. To have a little more strength.

"Look at me when I'm fucking you." He grips my cheeks and rips the side of my face up from the floor. "Look at me. I want to see you cry for me, baby." I feel him spit on my face, making me flinch.

Swallowing the bile that rises so I don't choke on it, I look up at him and spread my legs wider for him.

He pauses, his cock pushed inside me. Tilting his head, he gives my neck a little squeeze. "See, I knew you'd like it, you fucking whore." Leaning down, he runs his tongue across the tape that keeps me from telling him to go to hell. When he pulls away, he removes his hand from my face. And I realize this is my chance. "I'm going to fuck this cunt." He kisses my taped lips. "Then I'm going to fuck that ass—"

I lean up, ramming my face into his, causing my already busted face to bleed more.

"Fuck." He sits up, his hands flying to his face. "Bitch." He pulls his hands away to see they're now bloody.

I rise to a sitting position and do it again. My forehead hitting right on the bridge of his nose this time.

His cock slips out of me when he falls backward onto his ass.

My heart is racing, but this is it. My only chance. If I don't make it, he'll for sure kill me. But I refuse to go without a fight. I slam my foot into his neck, knocking him to the floor, and he starts coughing.

I stand on shaky legs and bend over. I slide my arms down over my ass and the back of my legs. Sitting on the edge of the couch, bent over, I slide them out from under my feet. They're still tied, but at least they're in front of me now. Jumping up from the couch, I run toward the kitchen. The bastard didn't tie my legs together. It's hard to rape a woman with her legs closed.

He reaches out and grabs my ankle, tripping me. A scream erupts from my taped lips as I land on my face.

"Fucking bitch!" he growls, yanking me back to him. My naked body slides across the cold tiled floor. "I'm going to keep you alive while I feed you to the fucking animals."

I reach out in front of me, trying to grab one of the power tools he knocked off the table, but they're too far away. I cry into the tape when his fingers dig into my skin. I can feel his nails clawing at my legs.

Turning over, I kick at him and manage to land a few to his face, and he lets go.

I crawl across the floor the best I can and reach what I need just as he flips me over. I lift the heavy orange nail gun and pull the trigger, but nothing happens.

He laughs at me. A deep rich laugh that makes his body shake, and my stomach sinks. "Really, Ray?" Falling to his knees, he straddles my hips, slapping my tied arms above my head. I hear the nail gun clank to the floor as his hands wrap around my throat once again. "You think that's going to save you?"

Panic grips my chest, and I do the only think I can think to do. Feeling around, I touch the nail gun and grab a hold of it and bring it up with all I have, slamming it into his already bloody face. Hard enough to knock him off me. I blink rapidly to clear my watery eyes and look at it in my hands once again. A green light blinks on the side. It has to work. I need …

"Fucking bitch!" He goes to yank it from my hands, but I press the trigger again, and he jumps back, screaming when it makes contact with his arm. "What the fuck?" Pulling his hand away, it's bloody.

Hope soars that I did it, and I take the opportunity to get to my feet. *What did I do different?* His wide eyes meet mine, and he charges me. I shove it into his chest and push it again. He stumbles back. His head drops while his hands feel around his chest. Fresh blood slowly starts to seep into his white T-shirt. "Bitch—"

I shove it into the side of his face and press again. He falls to his knees, screaming. If I could smile, I would. Standing behind him, I kick his back, shoving him facedown, and I bend over, pushing it into the back of his head and press the trigger five more times.

There's a loud sound coming from the gun, resembling a fan. I can barely hear it over the blood rushing in my ears. Taking a second, I stumble back and fall to my shaky knees, tears running down my face along with snot and sweat. He lies there motionless, and I hold my fingers over the trigger, ready to shoot him again if I need to.

I just need a second to regroup. To catch my breath. I'm suffocating with this duct tape on my face.

The front door opens, and I push myself up against the side of the couch as Mike enters.

"Holy shit." His wide eyes look over his house before they land on me.

I can't speak. The tape is too thick around my mouth for me to remove, and I'm not letting go of my only weapon. I'm still not even sure how to use it.

"You're okay," he says gently, his eyes falling to what I pray is a dead body that lays next to me. Swallowing, he blinks a few times. "I'll help you." I allow him to walk over to me. He reaches down to grab my arm, and I shove the end of the nail gun into his and press the trigger.

"Fuucckkkk." He retreats toward the kitchen. "Motherfucker," he mumbles, watching a thin line of blood run down his arm.

I pull my legs up to my chest, trying to cover my naked body from him while sniffling.

"I'll call Colt." He pulls his cell from his pocket. "Is that okay?" he asks me through gritted teeth.

I don't nod or shake my head because I can't. All that matters is that I keep the one weapon I have to survive. He's going to have to pry it from my restrained hands. And if I have to pull the trigger again, I won't stop until it's empty.

Thirteen

COLTON

THE GUYS AND I stand down in the basement of Blackout when Alex's cell rings.

"It's Mike." He frowns, looking up at me.

What the fuck does he want? None of us ever talk to him.

"Put it on speakerphone," Finn suggests.

Alex answers and holds it out so we can all hear. "Hello?"

"Hey, man. Is Colt with you?" he asks, sounding out of breath.

"What the fuck do you want, Mike?" I'm not in the mood for him right now. Especially after the morning I've had.

He grunts. "I have a situation here at my house."

"Why the fuck call me?" I demand, watching Tyson cut open a man who is strapped to a metal table. The body not even cold yet.

"Because it involves Raylee."

I yank the phone from Alex's hand. "What the fuck do you mean it involves Raylee?" As far as I know, they don't talk. I know this because I go through her cell sometimes. After what he did to her that night at his party, she's never cared much for him.

He takes in a few deep breaths and answers, "She's here."

Alex's eyes widen, and I grit my teeth. He has to be mistaken. Mike got released from jail earlier this morning and is already high. "Why would she be—?"

"You guys need to get here, and now," he interrupts me.

Finn is already grabbing our backpacks and shoving shit in them.

"How the fuck did she get there?" Alex demands.

But Mike ignores the question. "And Colt. She's going to need medical attention." He hangs up.

"What the fuck is going on?" Jenks asks.

"Let's go." I snap my fingers. *Medical attention?* What the fuck is going on? Why wouldn't he answer Alex on how she got there?

"Colt?" Tyson hollers my name as we go to leave the basement. We turn to look at him. "Bring her to the Cathedral. I'll call Gavin and meet you there. It'll save you time."

———————

"WHAT THE HELL is going on?" I demand, rushing into Mike's house but come to a stop at what I see.

Mike sits at the kitchen table, holding his right arm as blood runs down it, dripping on the floor. A man who looks like Nate is lying facedown on the tiled floor. Raylee sits up against the side of the couch next to him. Her knees pulled up to her chest. She's got her arms resting on them with a nail gun pointed at me. Duct tape is wrapped around her wrists, mouth, and head, and she's covered in blood.

The sight of her has my heart racing. My legs momentarily unable to move.

"What the fuck?" Finn whispers, entering behind me.

Blinking, I pull myself out of whatever daze I'm in and take a slow step toward her. "Princess..."

"Be careful, she'll shoot you," Mike warns, grunting.

I swallow and crouch down to her level, staying several feet away from her. "Hand me the nail gun, Raylee." I reach out my hand.

It starts shaking in her grasp, and I look over her busted face, wondering what the hell happened. How did she end up here? Tears silently run down the tape that covers her cheeks, and she sniffs. "Hand it to me, princess. And I'll remove the tape," I tell her.

"I think she's in shock," Finn states, looking her over.

Jenks moves to my right, and her eyes go to him. He throws his hands up and slowly walks over to the other side of Nate and

160

lowers himself, checking for a pulse. He shakes his head at us, and I swallow the knot that forms in my throat. Is this what Mitch tried to warn me about? I should have taken him seriously. But instead, I was blinded by my anger toward her.

She rejected me, so I ignored what could have prevented this.

"What the fuck happened?" Alex demands, removing his belt and securing it around Mike's arm to help stop the bleeding.

"I don't know. I just showed up, and they were like this. I tried to help her get the tape off her mouth, but she shot me."

Her watery eyes to go him, and they narrow.

"Raylee?" I demand, and they snap back to mine. "Hand me the nail gun." I reach out farther. I could rip it from her hands, but I don't want to do that. I want her to trust me enough to hand it over. Let her know that she has control of the situation. "Give it to me, princess. Come on. I'll get the tape off your mouth and your wrists, okay?" Whoever wrapped it around her face didn't intend to take it off. It starts under her chin and wraps all the way around right up to her nose.

The nail gun rattles in her grasp, but she closes her eyes and lowers it to the floor. I slide it out of the way, falling to my ass and pulling her onto my lap.

Her body shakes in mine while Finn walks over to us, pulling his pocketknife out and flipping it open. "It's okay. You're okay." I dig my fingers between her cheek and the tape, pulling it off her skin the best I can—it's on there pretty tight—and Finn slides the blade down it, cutting it away.

I yank it off as quick as I can, making her cry out, but some gets stuck in her hair. She sucks in a breath followed by a sob. I rip what's left off and push all the wet and matted hair from her face before grabbing her hands for Finn to cut that as well. She immediately wraps them around my neck once they're free.

"Someone find me a blanket," I bark out to anyone who is listening. Lowering my voice, I begin to rock her back and forth. "Shh." I run my hand down her bare back, and my teeth grind over the fact that she's fucking naked. My eyes catch sight of her shredded shirt, shorts, and underwear on the floor. I hold her trembling body tighter to me. "You're okay, princess. I got you. You're safe."

"Here." Alex comes over and drapes one across her body. I stand, lifting her into my arms.

"Colt?" I hear Finn call out behind me as I exit the house.

I spin around with her in my arms, giving him my attention.

His eyes go to Raylee hanging on to me for dear life with her face shoved into my chest before they meet mine. Coming face-to-face with me, he lowers his voice. "What do you want to do with Mike?"

"He was lying." I saw the way she looked at him when he said he just got home and found them here. I don't know why he would lie when he knows she knows the truth, but I'm going to find out. "Drive him in his car to the Cathedral. We'll take care of him afterward."

He nods. "Got it." Then turns and goes back inside.

I walk to the back of the Escalade SUV just as Alex exits the house. "Open this for me, please," I ask, nodding to the back hatch.

He rushes over and opens it up. I crawl in with her and stretch out my legs with her now on my lap, wanting to give her as much room as possible.

"Here, I grabbed her a water." He places it down next to me since my hands are full and closes the hatch. Once he jumps in the driver's seat, the vehicle comes to life and then starts backing up. "Jenks and Finn are making Mike help clean up and take care of Nate."

She flinches in my arms at the mention of his name while she continues to softly cry.

He goes on, "Then they're going to bring Mike to the Cathedral."

I nod, letting him know I'm listening, but I really don't give a fuck. I know my friends will make sure everything is taken care of.

Fourteen

COLTON

I MAKE MY way down the spiraling staircase and into the basement at the Cathedral with Alex on my ass. Tyson is already here along with Gavin, the doctor.

"She passed out on the way," I tell them, laying her unconscious body on a metal table. Her bloody face falls to the side. "I couldn't get her to wake up." Raising my hands, I shove my hair from my forehead, letting out a nervous breath.

She was sobbing one second, then out the next. I felt her body go slack in my arms, and I kept checking for a pulse, afraid she had died on me.

Alex called Tyson on the drive to fill them in on what we knew so the doctor knew what to expect.

Gavin points over to a tray and orders Tyson to grab something for him. After Tyson hands it off, I watch Gavin start an IV in her arm.

"I-I don't know ..."

"Take a breath." Tyson grabs my shoulders and pulls me back from the table. Placing his face in front of mine. "You brought her to get help. Now let her get the help, okay?"

I nod, stepping away from him, and his hands fall from my shoulders. I clench my fists while I watch Gavin open her eyes, flashing a light in them. He pulls the blanket down, exposing the top part of her body to the room. I haven't had a chance to look at her. She had her knees to her chest when we found her and then she was wrapped in a blanket on the way here. But she's got a bruise across her chest. "What is that from?" I ask, wondering out loud.

"Seat belt," the doctor answers.

I close my eyes and let out a sigh. *Her car.* Where the fuck was her car? It wasn't at Mike's, and neither was Nate's. There was a truck there, but I'm not sure whose it was. Finn had told me she ran out with a bag packed. She had left the house but somehow ended up at Mike's with Nate.

"Her neck?" I ask, looking at the bruises all over it.

He tilts her head back, frowning to get a better look. "I see handprints, but also looks like a ..." He pauses. "My best guess is a boot print."

"Your best guess?" I snap. *He fucking stepped on her?* Nate's lucky he's already fucking dead.

"Colt!" Tyson warns. "If you want to stay in here, then calm down."

Nodding again, I raise my hands at him so he doesn't knock my ass out. When he turns to talk to the doctor, I walk over to Alex, who stands silently in the corner, and pull out my cell, calling Finn.

"Hey, we're still here," he answers.

Good. "Go outside and tell me if you see her car." So much was going on that maybe I missed it.

"One sec." I hear a rustling of something before he answers. "No. Just a truck. I'll have Jenks run the plates ..." He trails off.

"Find something?" I ask.

"Yeah, could be nothing, but it's been wrecked. Back bumper." He sighs heavily. "It's got white paint on it."

"Finish up and get here." I hang up and look at Alex "Find her car," I order. "And when you do, make sure there's nothing left of it."

He nods.

"She was leaving our house going one of two places, our parents' or yours." His sister, Tatum, still lives with their parents, and for the first five miles, there would only be one road she'd take. But once she hits the highway, each one is in a different direction. I feel like he'd make sure to grab her before she made it to the highway. Too many eyes and people willing to stop and help if they see a wreck.

"On it." Then he's sprinting up the stairs and out of the basement.

Working for Tyson over the past year has taught us that you don't leave anything behind. Nothing that can give the cops a lead. I don't want anything out there that has to do with her. Her car popping up somewhere wrecked, then her being reported missing would be a problem.

Finding a chair, I sit in it and watch Gavin pull a cap off a syringe. I jump back to my feet. "What is that for?" I ask.

"Sedative," he answers.

"Why does she need that?" I want her awake. I need her to talk to me. Show me that she's okay. Tell me what the fuck happened.

He turns to face me. "I'm going to clean up the wounds before I stitch them. I don't want her waking up and becoming combative."

I walk over to the table, gritting my teeth. "She won't—"

"You don't know what happened to her," Tyson interrupts me. "Either he sedates her, or we tie her down for safety measures. Which do you prefer?" He arches a brow.

My chest tightens at that thought. She looked terrified when I found her at Mike's house. I'd hate for her to wake up restrained and get scared all over again. I told her she was okay. That I had her. Nodding, I sit back down in my chair and watch Gavin inject the medication into her IV.

RAYLEE

I FEEL LIKE I'm floating, and it's really warm. Everything seems foggy, and my tongue is heavy. I open my eyes and see bright lights, but images go in and out. Things are blurry all around, and there's a ringing in my ears.

"Where was it?" I hear what sounds like Colt's voice.

"I found it on the side of the road. Front end smashed. Airbags deployed." It's Alex who answers. "I recovered two cell phones, a purse, and her bag."

"Where is the car now?" Colt asks.

"Taken care of. And the truck also."

"Hello, Raylee." A man's blurry face appears above mine. "How do you feel? Any pain?" He shines a light in my eyes, and I try to blink, but he holds them open.

All I feel is high. Like I smoked a lot of weed and can't keep my eyes open. My skin feels clammy, and that ringing intensifies.

When I don't respond, he turns the light off. "The pain meds are doing their job."

"Where's Nate?" I hear Colt question.

I try to turn my head to look in the direction I hear the voices, but instead, my heavy eyes close.

"Finn has Mike helping bury him in the cemetery back behind the Cathedral," Jenks answers.

"Colt," the older man leaning over me calls out. "She's waking up."

I blink a few times, my eyes so heavy it's hard to keep them open. So I allow them to close. It could be two seconds, or it could be two hours before I open them again. Looking up, a set of green eyes are staring down at me. My vision is a little clearer now than before. "Hey, princess," Colt says softly.

I can't make my lips move to say anything. But I feel the sting of tears in my eyes.

"Don't cry," he whispers, reaching out and running his knuckles down the side of my face. "You're okay. You're safe now. It's over."

I try to open my mouth, but nothing comes out. Panic grips my chest that there's still tape on my face. My chest gets heavy, and I feel like I can't breathe.

"Raylee," Colt warns. "Raylee, stop." He's bent over me, holding both of my wrists in his hands.

I blink, confused. *Stop what?* I can't breathe. The tape. Get it off.

He yanks me to sit up, and the room sways while he pulls my legs to hang off the side of a table.

"Don't." He looks over my shoulder and snaps, "Don't. I'll calm her down." His eyes come back to mine. "Look at me, princess."

I blink again, clearing my vision, and he gives me a soft smile. "That's it. Breathe for me." He sucks in a deep breath, and I do the same. "The tape is gone."

I shake my head.

He nods. "Yes, it is. Feel." He lowers my heavy arms to my lap, and then I feel his warm hands on my neck. He runs them up my jawline and over my chin. Then cups my face. I lift my hands and place them over his. "See. It's gone."

I lick my lips and taste blood. Parting them again, I take in a deep breath.

"That's it." He smiles.

"Co … lt," I choke out.

"Yeah, it's me, princess."

My eyes dart around the large room. I see Alex and Jenks leaning up against a wall. Alex's arms are crossed over his chest while Jenks stares at me. I see the guy who held the light to my eyes dressed in a white lab coat. He's standing beside a guy I don't know who has his hands shoved into the pockets of his black dress slacks. My breathing picks up again, my pulse racing.

"Look at me." Colt brings my eyes back to his. "You're doing great, princess."

My teeth start to chatter, that warm feeling leaving me shivering, and I whisper, "I'm cold."

"Here." He pulls the blanket up and around my back, tucking it right under my chin and crossing it, pinning my arms inside. I wrap them around my stomach. "Better?"

I nod. "Thank you."

Leaning in, he kisses my forehead, and I sniff, trying to will my body to wake up. Where are we? How did I get here? The guy I'm assuming is a doctor said the pain medication was working. Is that why I feel numb and sluggish at the same time?

Someone clears their throat, and out of the corner of my eye, I see it's the older guy with the white coat on. "I need everyone to clear the room."

Colt stands to his full height, jaw sharp. "I'm not going anywhere."

The doctor walks over to us. "I need to speak to her," he argues.

"Then fucking speak," Colt snaps.

The doctor looks over at the man dressed in a button-up and slacks. He nods to the doctor, who then averts his eyes down to mine. "Raylee, I know this is hard. But with your consent, I'd like to have a sexual assault nurse examiner come in and see you. I can have her here in thirty minutes."

I feel Colt's body stiffen against my legs since he stands so close to me.

"There's no need," I say, swallowing the lump in my throat.

Colt lets out a long breath as if he was holding it in.

"I know this is hard," the doctor repeats. "But there could

have been drugs involved," he goes on. "You could have been unconscious—"

"I was awake when he started to rape me," I interrupt the doctor, and the room falls silent. Blood starts rushing in my ears. I'm glad I'm wrapped in the blanket because it helps shield the fact that my body is now trembling at having to admit that out loud. But I don't want a nurse to give me an exam. It won't do me any good. Nate is dead. I'm not going to be pressing charges.

"Started?" the man in the slacks asks, breaking the silence.

I nod and whisper, "I killed him before he could finish." At least I think I did. He was dead, right?

The doctor asks, "Did he use a condom?"

I lick my lips and taste the blood that still lingers. "I ... I don't know." I guess he could have put one on. I almost blacked out from him choking me right before. We always used them when we were dating. But as much as I was fighting, I can't see him taking the time to do that. The only person I've never used a condom with is Colt.

The older man looks from Colt to me. "There's always a chance of pregnancy—"

"I'm on the shot," I offer.

Silence falls over the room again and I look up at Colt. His green eyes are already on mine. A mask placed over his face, hiding how he feels for me right now, and my heart races at what he could be thinking.

I will not bow my head. I will not be ashamed of what Nate did to me. He tried to make me a victim. I turned myself into a survivor. That's nothing to be embarrassed about.

Fifteen

COLTON

S HE WOKE UP just like Gavin said she would—terrified. She was screaming that she couldn't breathe and to take the tape off her face. I don't even think she knew she was talking. In her mind, she was suffocating. He wanted to sedate her again, and I wasn't going to let that happen. What says she won't wake up the same way next time? I could calm her down and bring her back to here and now. Gavin had already removed her IV, and I wasn't going to help hold her down while he started another one.

When he asked us to clear the room, I was ready to body-slam him. Over my dead body will I leave her. I never thought it would be to talk about the possibility of Nate raping her.

I knew he did. The way her clothes were on the floor was all I needed to see. I tried to convince myself that it didn't happen, but deep down, I knew. He wanted revenge on my friends and me, and she was the easiest target. Or so he thought.

But the way she admitted it? In a room full of men with some she doesn't even know. It broke my heart while making me also see red that he did that to her. That he thought he could break her. But I know my girl. And she's a fighter.

She stares up at me, head held high, but there are tears in her pretty eyes. She's refusing to let them fall. Trying to be strong.

Stepping into her, I wrap my arms around her shoulders and hear her sniff. Her body shakes against mine, and I cup the back of her head, whispering in her ear, "I'm so sorry, princess."

"I'm—sorry," she whimpers.

I pull back, my hands on either side of her bruised face. The doctor stitched up the cuts, but the bruises will be there as a reminder for a while. "Don't. You have nothing to be sorry for. Do you understand me?"

Her pretty, crystal-blue eyes just stare up at me through watery lashes. Nothing that happened was her fault. It's mine, and there's nothing I can do to change that or make it better. Nate took something from her that can't be given back. And I wish he was still alive so I could kill him myself.

"Colt—"

The door opening behind me cuts her off, and I let go of her to turn and see Finn enter with Mike behind him. They're both covered in blood and dirt from digging Nate's grave.

"It's done." Finn slaps his hands together, knocking off some dirt. He looks at Raylee. "A nail gun?" He arches a brow with a smirk on his face, not knowing what she just confessed to all of us.

"It was the closest thing I could reach." She wipes the tears from her face, trying to calm herself.

He laughs. "God, I never want to piss you off."

Mike comes to a stop when his eyes meet hers. He hasn't said shit about what went down, and I haven't questioned him. I wanted her awake and coherent. She's the only one who can tell us what he's lying about and why. His eyes drop to the floor while silence lingers in the room. Running his hand through his hair, he shuffles from foot to foot. "I better get going." Mike turns to head to the door.

Alex steps in front of it and leans his back on it. "Not yet. There're still some things to iron out."

Mike raises his hands in surrender. "I promise I won't say anything."

I look over at Tyson, and he shrugs. It's up to me if I let Mike walk away from this. What he's seen. What he knows. I know he won't run his mouth about what Raylee did to Nate. Finn had Mike help him dispose of the body for a reason. Mike would never tell on himself. No. He's smarter than that. His fate will depend on what Raylee has to tell us.

"We're not worried about that," Alex tells him.

"Guys, come on." Mike gives a nervous laugh. "I—"

"What's a Lord?" Raylee asks, interrupting him.

I spin around to face her as the room falls silent. She looks up at me expectantly.

"What did you say?" Jenks asks her, pushing away from the wall.

"A Lord? What is it?"

I go to lie but stop myself. I've never told her who I work for or what I do. She just thinks she knows. So for her to ask this question means she's been told something. So I keep my mouth shut and see what else she has to say.

Her eyes dart around the room before meeting mine again. "Mike told Nate that you guys worked for the Lords. That you guys kill for a living." Her voice doesn't waver in the slightest at her words. It's like she almost expected it.

Mike starts to fight Alex, trying to get out the door, but Alex just pushes him farther back into the room. "How do you know about the Lords?" he demands to Mike.

Finn throws his hands up, facing Tyson. "I didn't say shit," he rushes out. Remembering the threat that Tyson gave us when he brought us on to work for him.

Tyson smirks. "Mike knows about the Lords because he was one once. Weren't you, Mike?"

Mike slowly turns around to face the room but says nothing.

"But he couldn't keep his nose clean," Tyson adds. "When Barrington kicked him out, so did the Lords."

This is interesting. "So Mitch ...?"

"He's not a Lord." Mike spits out. "He wanted nothing to do with them."

Finn scratches the back of his head. "Wait ... when we arrived at your house, you said you had found them like that. Nate was dead. But Raylee just said that you spoke to Nate."

His eyes widen, realizing that she just told on him. I step in front of her, blocking her from his view in case he decides to come for her. "He was dead." Mike growls. "She killed him."

Raylee reaches out and shoves me to the side, standing from the table. She stumbles on wobbly legs and pushes me away when I go to help her. She wraps the blanket around her shoulders, shielding her still naked body. "I heard everything," she tells him, lifting her chin.

"No. She's making shit up." He starts laughing.

"Funny." Finn smiles. "Nate said the same thing about her." He refers to when we were back at the house last night, and Nate was calling her a liar when she said he was forcing her to leave with him. "He was also the one who was lying," Finn adds.

Mike shakes his head quickly. "No. No. I'm telling the truth."

"I heard you," she argues.

"No!" he shouts, running his hands through his hair. His eyes dart around the room quickly. What the fuck did she hear that's got him on edge? He lowers his voice and mumbles more to himself than anything else. "You were unconscious."

"I was pretending." She gives a rough laugh. "You told Nate that I wasn't worth it. That I'm Colt's whore. And that he's destroyed every relationship I've ever had." Taking another step closer to him, I grab her shoulders, keeping her in place. The need to protect her is strong, but I don't want to hurt her. She's already been injured enough. "Nate was going to let you have a piece of me. And after you guys were done with me, you'd cut me up and dump my body in the woods. Let the animals eat what was left of me."

"You what?" I growl, stepping in front of her. He was going to kill her? Dump her body in the woods? My pulse races at the thought of anyone doing her any harm, let alone taking her away from me completely. I fucking love this woman, and I swear on my life that no one is going to hurt her ever again. I was dumb enough to let her walk away from me this morning. That'll never happen again.

"No." He places his hands up. "I never said that. Nate said that."

"Then you left me there with him. Said you had to meet someone in fifteen minutes. Told him not to touch me until you got back."

I charge him.

"Colt—"

My fist clocks him in the face before he can finish whatever bullshit he was going to say. "Alex." I growl his name and he removes his belt. He leans down, wrapping it around Mike's neck, yanking him to his feet and holding Mike's back to his front, choking him.

I look over to see that she's now standing next to me. Angry tears fall from her eyes. "You told him that you didn't want him doing anything that couldn't be covered up. That you didn't want cops at your house because they found a dead body in the woods with a blood trail leading back to your place. And to sit down, have a drink, and wait. That when you returned, you'd come up with a plan together."

I fist my busted hand, getting ready to hit him again. It's been a while since any of us killed a guy with our fists. That's how we got this job in the first place.

"I didn't stay gone," he grinds out, trying to pull the belt from his neck but there's no use. Alex has it pulled tight. "I came back … to check on you. I knew Nate wouldn't wait. I didn't want him to hurt you—"

"Hurt me?" She laughs roughly. "He wanted to kill me!" she screams, stepping into him. "And you knew that."

"But he didn't—"

"He fucking slammed my face into the coffee table. Several times. Slapped me, choked me. Raped me." She reaches up and slaps him. "How does that feel?" She slaps him again. "Does it fucking hurt?" She drops the blanket and steps even closer, kneeing him in the balls.

Alex lets go of the belt around Mike's neck, and he falls to the floor, holding himself while he curls up into a ball.

I grab the blanket and wrap it around her from behind and pick her up with my arms around her waist while she kicks her legs out, trying to make contact with him.

"Calm down," I say, carrying her over to a chair and sitting her in it. I kneel before her, reaching up and pushing some hair from her face. "Take a deep breath." I don't want her to hurt herself. She's already been through so much and needs rest.

"He left me there with him." Her watery eyes meet mine. "He … left me." Tears spill down her bruised cheeks, and my chest tightens at the crack in her voice.

"He'll pay for that. I promise," I assure her.

Mike laughs, sitting up, and I look over at him. "And you? Who the fuck is going to make you pay, Colt?" He looks around the room. "All of you. You guys humiliated him. You didn't think he'd go after her?" He snorts. "I would have done the same."

Alex kicks him in the face, knocking his head back, and he falls to the floor, out cold. "Want to take care of him now?"

"No," I answer Alex. She deserves to have her revenge and she's nowhere near physically ready for that. "Not yet."

"I'll keep him at Blackout," Tyson states. "Just let me know when and I can deliver him wherever you want."

I nod. "Thank you." Looking back down at her, I cup her face, wanting to get her as far away from here as possible, away from everyone. "Let's go home."

RAYLEE

I WALK UP the stairs to our house that we all share and make it to the top. I stand here for a few seconds, debating on what to do. Colt's room is to the right. Mine to the left. I don't want to be alone right now. Left with my thoughts.

Thankfully, like always, Colt makes the decision for me. He grabs my hand and ushers me to his room. Stepping inside, he closes the door behind him. Walking to the other side of his room, he opens the door to his bathroom, and I hear him start the bathtub.

I enter his bathroom and remove the blanket that I have wrapped around me. I've got bruises all over. Some you can tell are from the car wreck, others from Nate. The doctor gave me some medication to fight infection and STDs. He said I needed to be seen again in a couple of weeks for a follow-up.

Whatever pain meds he gave me have worn off, and I feel like shit. Or maybe it was the adrenaline spike after I woke up and saw Mike. I lied to the doctor and pretended to feel good, not wanting to be high anymore. I'd rather feel pain than be numb.

Colt turns and reaches out to me. I take his hand, and he helps me step into the corner Jacuzzi tub. Sinking down into the hot water, I look up at him. He's grabbing me a towel out of the cabinet and lays it down next to the tub.

"Was it true?" I ask. We haven't spoken since we left … wherever we were. It wasn't a real hospital, but it looked like one on the inside.

He pauses and looks down at me. His eyes give nothing away, but they never do. I never could figure him out. That's why I always felt so lost. Because he hid everything but hatred from me so well.

The silence lingers while I wait for him to answer. Technically, I just asked two questions. Did he ruin every relationship I ever had, and does he kill people for a living? I'm curious to see which one he chooses to answer. I felt that was my only chance to know who or what a Lord was while also outing Mike at the same time.

Colt looks away first. "Yes."

I run my hands through the warm water, cupping it and pouring it on my chest while the faucet continues to fill the large tub. "Which one?"

"Both."

"Why?" I whisper, my eyes dropping to the water to see it's dirty from the blood that's washed off.

He sits on the side of the tub, letting out a sigh. "Because I love you."

My chest squeezes at his answer, and my eyes snap to his. I always thought he had something to do with my lack of love life. But I thought it was because he just wanted to make my life miserable. I might have hated him as much as I thought he hated me, but I never ruined any of his relationships. But then again, he never had any. In the six years I've known Colton Knox, he's never had a girlfriend. "Colt—"

"I always have," he interrupts me. "Since the moment I saw you in my father's kitchen."

I'm not sure at what point I allowed myself to feel anything for him, but even when we were at each other's throats, I could never see my life without him. I hate that we've come so far, only for Nate to ruin it. "And now?" Tears spring to my eyes, my pulse racing, knowing he's going to reject me.

He frowns, tilting his head to the side.

"How do you feel about me now?" My throat closes up on me. "After Nate …" I can't get the words out this time.

When he stands, my heart starts pounding in my chest that he's going to walk away. But instead of leaving, he rips his shirt up and over his head and undoes his jeans. Toeing off his shoes and removing his socks, he shoves his jeans and black boxer briefs down his legs and kicks them away before stepping into the water. I lean up from the tub and he sits down behind me.

Wrapping his arms around my shaking shoulders, he pulls my back into his chest. "Nothing …" he whispers in my ear. "Nothing could ever make me not love you, princess."

The first tear runs down my face and I nod, sniffling. I lean my head on his chest, taking in a shaky breath.

"Don't think that what Nate did to you makes me see you any differently." He pulls all of my hair off my chest and back, placing it over my left shoulder. "You were my princess then. And you're my princess now." Sighing, he adds, "I'm sorry I wasn't there for you. I'm sorry that he came after you."

I pull away from him and turn off the water before it gets too high. Turning in the tub, I look over at him. "It wasn't your fault."

"It was." He sits up. "Me and the guys—"

"I let you do those things to me, Colt. I …" I drop my eyes to the dirty water. "I wanted it." I may not remember everything that happened at Mike's house. But I remember what he said to me in the bedroom and how turned on I got. I willingly followed him back into the party, knowing that he was going to do something to me, and I was going to beg for it. I've never told him no or to stop. I willingly let him have his way with me because I want him to. Nate saw an opportunity and took advantage of it. Of me. He used Colt and the guys as an excuse to be a raping murderer.

"Hey." He cups my chin gently, forcing my eyes back up to his. "Don't feel guilty."

Biting my bottom lip, I look away from him and stare at the black tiled wall as if it holds all the answers to the questions that I want to ask.

He scoots closer to me, and I feel my throat close up on me. I hate feeling this way. I told myself that what Nate did wasn't going to affect me. That I wouldn't allow him to win. Colt just confessed he loves me and all I can do is think that I've ruined what we could have had.

"Look at me, princess."

The sorrow in his voice pulls my eyes back to his. I blink, and fresh tears run down my face.

"We'll take it one day at a time, okay?" he offers, and I nod slowly. "I'm going to be right here with you." Lifting my hand, he kisses my busted knuckles that I got from the car wreck. "And I promise, no one will hurt you again."

"Thank you," I manage to whisper, and he sighs.

I believe him. That's one thing about Colt, he keeps his promises. Over the past six years, if he said he was going to do something, then he did it. I want him to love me for me. The me before today. The one before Nate came along and tried to ruin me for anyone else. I refuse to let that sorry bastard win. I will have my happy ending with the man I love. No matter how far I have to push myself to get it.

Sixteen

COLTON

I EXIT THE bathroom for her to finish up in the tub when I hear a knock on my bedroom door. I tighten the towel around my hips, tying it off, and open the door to see Finn standing there.

"I thought you might want this." He offers me a cell phone.

"Why does this look familiar?" I wonder out loud. It's in a simple black case. Alex already gave me the two he found in her car. We knew one was hers, and the other was Tatum's. Why would I want this one too?

"Because it was Nate's," he answers.

Looking up at him, I frown. "How did you get it?"

"I found it at Mike's. I didn't want to give it to you in front of the guys. But I thought you'd want to see what's on it."

I fist it in my hands. "See what's on it? What the fuck does he have? Is it naked pictures of her from when they were dating?" That's the last thing I want to fucking look at.

He shakes his head. "He recorded it."

My stomach sinks, the blood rushing from my face. Just when I thought it couldn't get any worse. The motherfucking bastard recorded it.

"She hasn't told you?" he questions, noticing my reaction.

"Why would she tell me that?" I growl.

He sighs heavily. "She was aware, Colt. It wasn't like he had it hidden in the house."

Nate is lucky that she killed him. I would have made it very slow and very painful.

He goes on at my silence, "I'm guessing he was going to send it to you. You know, since all of this started with your sex tape."

My teeth grind at the fact I did this to her. Every little fucking thing I've done because I was a jealous little bitch led to this very second. I'd give my life if I could take it all away for her. If I had just chased her down after my call with Mitch. I could have prevented all of this. "Did you watch it?" I clear my throat.

He nods, and his eyes soften. "Yeah." They look over to my closed bathroom door and then back to mine. "She put up one hell of a fight." Running his hand through his hair awkwardly, he adds, "It's fucked up, I know. But if it were me, I'd want to know." Slapping the doorway, he takes a step back into the hall. "I broke into it and removed the code access needed."

"We'll go through it tomorrow. No telling what else is on here," I grind out. We need to find out who that truck belongs to. They're going to question where it went and why Nate hasn't returned it.

"I didn't go through it, but I did check his last incoming message. Mike had texted him."

"And?"

"He was turning around and heading back. Told Nate that he was all in and they could take Raylee to his parents' cabin. It's like an hour away, and they could play with her as long as they wanted. No one would think twice to look for her there."

He's wrong. I would have found her. The question is how long would I have waited to look for her?

"I think him walking in on Nate dead scared him. He thought he could call you and get away with it. Especially after what he told us earlier. He thought she was unconscious, so he never expected her to tell us the truth."

Over my dead body will he get away with this. "Thanks again."

He nods and then walks away.

I hear the bathroom door open, and I quickly open the top drawer to my dresser and stick the phone under my boxers, so she won't find it. I'll watch it later after she's asleep. Turning around, I see her standing in the doorway of the bathroom.

She's got scratch marks up and down her calves and stitches in her face. A part of the bruise from the seat belt is noticeable, the rest of it is currently hidden by the towel that's wrapped underneath her arms. Her neck shows he tried to choke her. I've always been rough with our sex, but I've never made her look like I physically abuse her.

Pushing off the doorway, she drops the towel. *She's testing me.* To see what I'll do. If I'll treat her different. I wasn't lying to her. My feelings about her haven't changed, but that doesn't mean I'm going to tie her to my bed and beat her ass with my belt while I fuck her mouth. Her body needs time to recover. And who knows how she'll react if I were to actually put my hands on her. Will she see me as Nate? Will she freeze up? Try to kill me? Either one is very possible.

She walks over to where I stand, and I allow her to remove the towel from my hips. Her eyes drop to my hard dick, and my teeth clench. Of course, I'm hard. I'm in love with this woman, and she's standing in front of me naked.

"Colt," she whispers my name. "Please?"

I look down at her. "I don't think …"

My words trail off when she grabs my hands and places them on her large breasts. "I want you, Colt." Leaning up on her tiptoes, she plants a soft kiss on my lips, and it takes everything in me not to return it.

I can't hold back the groan when her tongue runs across my lips. My thumbs brush over her nipples on their own, feeling them harden with my touch.

Pulling back, I see the internal battle she's fighting within herself. The want to not let Nate win and the fear that she'll no longer be the same woman she was.

"I don't want him to be the last man to touch me," she whispers.

My chest tightens at her words. That I didn't save her. How can she ever trust me again? I'm not going to hide anything from her ever again. If she wants to know something, all she has to do is ask. Hell, she knows I kill for a living now and is still here with me.

"Please, Colt?" Her bottom lip trembles at my silence. "Remind me that I'm yours."

Gently cupping her face, I bend down and take her lips with mine. She opens up for me, and I taste the tears she cried while in the bathtub. I hate that they make my cock twitch.

I didn't realize that she was training me while I was training her all these years. What she needs is what I need. It's why every other woman hasn't been able to compare to her.

Pulling away, I lay my forehead on hers, taking in a deep

breath. I jump when I feel her hand wrap around my dick. She runs it up and down my long shaft. "Princess," I whisper, trying to fight the urge to pick her up by her ass and throw her onto my bed.

"Please," she begs, gripping me tighter. "Please, Colt." Her voice trembles.

"I don't want to hurt you." Even as I say the words, my hands come up and tangle in her wet hair, pulling her head back gently so I can look down into her eyes.

"I want you to," she chokes out as her tears spill over. "I-I need you."

I shake my head, knowing I won't be able to turn her down.

She releases my dick, and I let out the breath I'd been holding in, but my relief is quickly replaced with something else when she drops to her knees. "Raylee," I growl, pulling on her hair to lift her up, but she swats my hands away since I didn't have a tight enough grip and takes my cock into her mouth. "Raylee," I snap, getting angry with myself.

Getting to her feet, she slaps me. "Don't call me that, *Colton.*" She uses my full name.

"Ray—"

She slaps me again, and I grip her chin, my eyes narrowing down on her. The look of fucking triumph crosses her pretty features, and I hate that it makes me want to wipe it off her face.

We've always gone toe-to-toe with one another. She knows what to do and exactly what to say to push me. "Don't make me—"

"Make you what?" She licks her busted lip.

My body trembles with the need to dominate while rocking her to sleep. I've never wanted to hurt her and cocoon her in Bubble Wrap at the same time.

"Show me who you are, Colt. Remind me what I am." She runs her nails down my chest, cutting my skin, and I grind my teeth.

"You're letting him win," I growl, and her body goes stiff against mine.

"No. You're letting him win," she argues, shoving my hand from her chin. "You're treating me like I'm broken. As if I don't know what I want." Her hand connects with my face again, and my cheek is now on fire. "You're fucking weak!" she screams.

I grip her wrists in my hands to keep her from hitting me anymore, and she whimpers, but her eyes tell me she's not going to stop. "I'm not—"

"You said you love me." Tears fall from her pretty eyes, and she yanks her hands free from my loosened grip. I'm trying my best not to hurt her.

"I do."

"Another lie!" she shouts. "I'm just a game to you. You don't give a fuck …" Her hand slaps my face once more, and I've had enough.

Stepping into her, I grab her ass and lift her off the floor. I walk over to the bed and toss her onto it. Settling between her parted legs, I take my cock into my hand and press into her cunt. Not even checking to see if she's ready.

A cry rips through the room when we both realize she's not as wet as usual. I'm not going to use a condom with her. I never have before, and I'm not going to start now just because Nate raped her. I want her to know that things are the same. That I still want her and need her like I always have.

"Is this what you want, princess?" I growl, placing my hands behind her knees and spreading them wide open. Pulling back, I slam forward, making her tits bounce.

She covers her face with her hands, muffling her cries. I let go of her legs and pin her upper arms down to the bed instead, ripping her hands from her face. "Look at me, princess," I demand. My heart is pounding, and my pulse is racing at what she's feeling right now. Why she's making me do this. Why she's going to push herself so far, so soon.

When she opens her eyes, tears spill down the side of her face. I always want her begging for me with mascara streaks running down her gorgeous face, but it's different. I never want to see her like this. "What are you?" I ask her, softening my voice.

She shakes her head, sniffing.

I squeeze her arms harder and growl, "Tell me." Lowering my face to her neck, I pull my hips back and then push forward, going slow but deep. Her pussy gets wetter with each thrust. "Tell me that you're my good little slut and that you want me to make you come all over my dick."

She chokes out a sob, and I bite down on her skin.

"Please?" she cries.

My chest tightens at the single word. She's never sounded this desperate before, but I can't break. She needs me to be strong and give her what she wants, so I'm going to do it. "You know the rules. You want it, you have to beg for it."

"I'm—" I feel her swallow against my lips. "I'm your good little slut," she whimpers, admitting it. "Please make me come … all over your dick."

"Good girl," I whisper, but don't let up. "You're my good little slut, princess." I lean up just enough to take her lips with mine. I kiss her. Dominating her mouth, letting her feel my love, my hate, my fucking regret. I pour everything I have into it, hoping that she understands that I love her, and I'll do anything for her.

When I pull away, we're both panting. "Look at me. Eyes on me." I tell her while I fuck her into my mattress, holding her down. I don't want her closing her eyes and seeing Nate.

I slam into her, almost as if I hate her. But I don't. Not anymore. And honestly, I don't think I ever did. I've heard people say it's hard to pinpoint the exact second you fall in love with someone. I'm pretty sure it was the moment I first saw her. And I've been falling ever since.

She fights me but doesn't tell me to stop. She's still crying, her eyes on mine, and I watch them grow heavier with each thrust as the headboard bangs against the wall.

"That's it. Come all over my dick, princess. That's what a good slut does." My words tip her over the edge, and her pussy clamps down on me. She arches her back. Sweat covers both of our bodies, and she sobs while coming.

The moment she gets off, I pull out and let go of her, sitting up. She pulls her legs to her chest and rolls onto her side, covering her face with her hands, trying to muffle her cries.

I lie down and stretch out in front of her. Wrapping my arms around her trembling body, I pull her into me. "You're okay," I say, holding her tightly. "I'm so sorry, princess." I apologize for giving her what she wanted.

I knew it wasn't going to be easy for her. But she wanted me to push her. Raylee is the type of woman who wants to appear strong, no matter what it costs.

"You did so good." I kiss her sweat-covered skin.

Pulling her head from my chest, she places her lips on mine. I cup her face and gently kiss her back. "It's me," I say against her wet lips. "It's me, princess. I got you." I can't even begin to imagine how she feels right now. But I know that I will do whatever she needs me to do for her.

Her bloodshot eyes search mine. "I'm … sorry." She chokes

on her words.

"You have nothing to be sorry for." I hate that she apologizes for what she feels. That something in the back of her mind is telling her she's in the wrong.

Licking her lips, she whispers, "I love you, Colt." Fresh tears fall from her eyes, and I wipe them away. "I love you."

I open my mouth, but she buries her head into my chest again, sobbing.

Epilogue
COLTON

I STAND SURROUNDED by woods back behind the Cathedral in the cemetery—it's the Lords' personal burial ground. Raylee stands about ten feet in front of me, her large sunglasses on her face as the sun starts to rise over the tall trees. It's not quite that bright yet, but she wears them to cover up the bruises from Nate. They're not as bad as they were, but still noticeable.

She turns, giving me a profile view, and smiles at something Alex says to her. It's a real one. Over the past week, I've seen her fake it.

Last night, I woke up in bed alone and found her on the couch. The moment she saw me, she wiped her eyes and put a smile on her face. Like she thinks I don't know the difference.

I'm not going to call her out on it, though. When I asked her what she was doing, she told me she couldn't sleep and wanted to watch TV but didn't want to wake me. I carried her back to our room, laid her in bed, and turned on the TV. She fell asleep in my arms before the movie even started while I ended up staying awake the rest of the night.

I catch sight of Finn walking over to me. "How's the hand?" he asks so only I can hear.

I look down and stretch out my fingers before making a fist. "Getting better."

"You okay?" he asks.

"Yeah." I nod. After Raylee told me she loved me, she passed out almost instantly, crying herself to sleep. I waited for a few minutes, grabbed Nate's phone out of the drawer, and went downstairs to watch the video.

I don't know what my sick mind thought I'd see, but I was not prepared.

Afterward, I went a little crazy. Broke some shit and punched a wall. Finn found me sitting in the dark and tried to calm me down, but there was nothing he could do. I still hear the words echo in my head.

"Tell Colt that you're my dirty fucking slut now."

"Tell him how much you're going to enjoy me tying you down and letting my friends fuck you."

"They're going to use you like the whore you are, baby."

"Beg him now!"

"Huh, you fucking whore. Beg Colt to fuck you now."

It made me sick to my stomach. But Finn was right. She fought hard. I watched it, holding my breath. Even though I knew she was in our bed upstairs asleep, I kept waiting for her to close her eyes and not open them again. I didn't tell her I watched it, but I think she knew something was up the next morning.

"What happened to your hand?" she asks, looking down at it.

It's swollen to the point I can't even make a fist, covered in cuts and bruises.

"Jesus, Colt," she whispers at my silence. "It looks broken. You should see the doctor."

"I'm fine." I brush off her concern. How can she even be worried about me? It's just a hand. It'll heal.

"What did you do?" she goes on.

"I did it when I hit Mike," I lie. The way her brows pull down, I know she's having a hard time believing it. I'm not going to tell her I watched the video and went ballistic in the living room. She hasn't even mentioned it to me that Nate was recording them. She doesn't want me to know a video of that exists. I don't blame her. "Come on. You need to eat breakfast and take your pain pills."

"I don't need them." She drops her eyes to the floor, and I step into her.

"You need to take them." I know her. If she doesn't take the pills

192

and relax, she'll do too much. Hurt herself even more. Thankfully, Gavin said nothing was broken, but that doesn't mean she's not in pain right now. Especially after what I did to her last night when we got back from the Cathedral.

She crosses her arms over her chest. "I'll take them when you see the doctor about your hand."

"Doesn't work that way, princess."

We make our way downstairs to the kitchen, and all the guys are already at the table. Jenks leans under it and kicks the chair out across from him for her to sit on.

"Aren't you a gentleman?" Finn laughs.

"I have my moments." He shrugs.

"I'm going to go use the restroom," Raylee announces and walks down the hall.

I almost ask if she needs me to go with her but decide against it. She doesn't like to be coddled. After the way she started a fight with me last night, I know she already thinks I'm treating her differently after what happened. And now that I've seen the video, I'm not sure that I can treat her any other way. I declared my love for her. She's my responsibility. I have to protect her.

She returns, sitting down in the seat next to me. I reach over, gripping one of the legs with my good hand and pull her closer to my side. Reaching forward, I grab the cereal and milk that the guys have out and start to pour her a bowl.

"What happened in the living room?" she asks.

"Alex," Finn answers quickly before anyone else can rat me out. "He got mad at his ex."

"That's why she's an ex." Alex laughs, playing along. "Always pissing me off."

Raylee nods once. "Yeah, I was going to call Raven yesterday before …" Nate kidnapped and raped her. "To check in. I'm worried about her."

Alex sits up straighter, placing his forearms on the table. "Worried how?"

She shrugs. "Could be nothing, but Rick gave me the creeps. Tatum too."

"Who the fuck is Rick?" Alex snaps.

"Uh…" She nibbles nervously on her busted bottom lip. "He was at Mitch's party with her…"

"Goddammit," he growls, snatching his phone off the table and storming out of the kitchen.

"How's she doing?" Finn asks, getting my attention.

I sigh. How do I respond to that? She's the same but different. She's been starting fights with me over the past week. Often. I see them coming a mile away. She starts to shut down before my eyes. Then the next thing I know, she's yelling at me, wanting a fight. Physically pushing me to the point I have to remind her whose name is carved into her ass.

She wants our sex rough. More than it ever has been, which is hard, considering she's still healing. Every time, she cries during, sobs afterward, and then she's better. It's almost as if the sex is therapeutic for her. Her way of coping. I hate it, but I'd do anything for her. We fucked three times just yesterday alone.

"Good," I finally say.

"It'll get better." He slaps my back as if he doesn't believe my answer.

I don't pretend to understand what she went through but watching the video gave me a better idea as to why she wanted me to fuck her. Why she needed me to remind her she belonged to me. Nate took something from her that she's trying to get back. Raylee is stubborn, and she's going to do whatever has to be done to prove to herself that she's still the same Raylee. Even if that means pushing herself past her own limits.

She says something to Jenks, and my eyes fall on her once again. She's dressed in one of my black hoodies, black skinny jeans, and black boots. Her bleach-blond hair is up in a messy bun, and she's pushed her sunglasses to sit on top of her head.

We're having dinner at our parents' house next weekend. Raylee said by then she should be able to cover up what's left of the bruising with makeup. I've decided I'm going to tell them about us. She doesn't know it, and she may get mad at me, but I don't care. I've kept her a secret long enough. I want to be the man she deserves, and that's someone who is proud to love her. And if anyone disagrees with us being together, then fuck them. Her feelings are the only ones that matter to me.

RAYLEE

I TURN, LOOKING over my shoulder to see Colt talking to Finn. They look to be in a deep conversation. Their words are too hushed for me to hear what it's about.

I've been pushing him more and more every day over the past week. More so than I ever have before. I think he really wants to kill me, but I'm not going to let up on him.

I love him, and he loves me.

I never expected my love to match my hatred for him. I thought the game of who can destroy the other was what would do us in. *But love?* That's the deadliest kind of drug. I realized that day in his room after we got back from the Cathedral that his love for me can force him to do things against his will.

It gives me more power than I ever had.

Apart, we were our own worst enemy, but together? We're explosive. An unbeatable team.

I haven't apologized for setting his car on fire, and I never will. The stupid bastard should have never recorded us, let alone shared it on social media. Plus, I'm sure he'll piss me off at some point, and I'll set something else of his on fire.

"Have you spoken to Raven?" I ask Alex, placing my attention back on him.

He shakes his head. "Nope. She won't answer my phone calls or return my texts."

I'll text her tomorrow. I've stayed hidden at the house with Colt. I haven't even seen Tatum. Not until the stitches are out of my face and the bruises are faded more. Not wanting to have to talk about what happened. I want to move on. And it'll be harder if I have to talk about it every day.

I feel a set of hands on my shoulders, and I jump. "Ready?" Colt whispers in my ear from behind me.

I nod, thankful he doesn't acknowledge my unease. What Nate took from me isn't going to return overnight, but I'm determined to move on and not let that fucker control my life. Right now, I feel good. It's been a long week, but I'm healing. Like Colt said—one day at a time.

Colt kisses my cheek, and I feel him pull away, stepping back. Letting me know I can do this on my own, but all I have to do is say the word, and he'll take over for me.

A man who I now know by the name of Tyson walks into my line of sight. I sat down with him, Colt, and the guys a couple of nights ago in his office at his club Blackout. Colt told me I could ask whatever I wanted, and they would answer it. I learned that night that I had been living with four men who have very dark secrets. It should have made me run away from him, but instead, it made me love Colt even more. Nothing about our past together has ever not been complicated. Besides, Colt has seen me at my worst, and he still chose me. I'll always choose him too. No matter what he does.

"Here you go," Tyson announces, dragging Mike behind him by the rope that is wrapped around his wrists. He's got duct tape wrapped all the way around his mouth and head, like Nate did to me.

Tyson brings him to a tree and throws the rope over a limb before tying it off, securing Mike to it with his hands above his head. His shoes barely touch the ground.

Finn steps in front of me with a smirk playing on his lips. "Give him hell, Ray." He holds out a Paslode XP nail gun. The same one I used on Nate. He gave me a crash course on it a few days ago. Turns out, the damn thing has some kind of safety. And it only shoots nails when it's pressed up against the target. Or you can pull the slide back. But I didn't have that luxury with my wrists tied together. I didn't know what I did to make it work last time. I'm just glad I know how to work it now. Winking at me, he adds, "I've been charging it for you. It's loaded with fifty nails. Ready for you to use. And I brought plenty more." He nods to his backpack on the ground by his feet.

The sound of Mike screaming behind his gag makes me smile. "Thanks, Finn."

I take it in my hands, and it seems even heavier than that day at Mike's. My heart is racing but not like it was then. This is a different kind of adrenaline. There's a calmness when it comes to revenge. I know what I'm doing isn't any better than him, but I just don't give a fuck.

I've always had that kind of attitude, but now I only care about one thing—Colt. He allows me to pull him into the darkness so I can bathe in the light. And I do the same for him.

But Mike deserves to know what it feels like to be helpless. To have no hope of anyone coming to save him. To be humiliated.

"Hey, Finn?" I turn to face him on my right. He's the closest to me. Everyone else stands behind us.

"Yeah, gorgeous?" he asks.

"Do you have your pocketknife on you?"

"Always." He pulls it from his pocket and flips it open. "Want to carve him up first?"

I shake my head. "Will you remove his shirt?"

Mike starts thrashing, twisting his body around and kicking his legs out, forcing me to take a step back so they don't hit me. Finn punches him in the stomach, making him hunch over the best he can with his hands tied above his head. Then Finn starts cutting the T-shirt off his body. Once done, he closes the knife. "All yours."

"Hold this for a sec." I offer him the nail gun and he takes it. I undo Mike's belt and unfasten his jeans. I rip them down his legs along with his boxers to his ankles and fasten the belt, tying his legs together.

I want to humiliate him. Plus, it keeps him from kicking his legs out at me.

"Thanks." I reach out, taking the nail gun back.

"My pleasure." Finn smirks.

Mike is screaming, his chest heaving. He throws his head back, looking up at his tied arms as if he can come up with a way to save himself. It's not going to happen.

Lifting the nail gun, I hold it against the side of his flaccid dick. He stills, body going stiff. I look up into his wide eyes and pull the trigger. He screams so loud behind the tape that the birds fly out of the surrounding trees. "I know how much you hate blood on your dick," I say, tilting my head to the side. I make fun of the fact he stopped fucking me after he learned I was a virgin. Even though I know it was because of his fear of Colt.

I hear a gagging noise behind me and turn around to see Alex bent over, his hands on his knees trying not to vomit. Finn is smiling, nodding his head. Jenks is rubbing Alex's back. "Dude, you kill for a fucking living."

Alex shakes his head and stands upright, crossing his legs with his hand over his dick like he's next.

I look at Colt, who is staring at me intently. He's got his legs wide, and arms crossed over his chest. He arches a brow as if to ask me if I need help, and I give him a smile.

I can do it myself.

Turning back to Mike, I shove the jagged edge into his thigh and pull the trigger. His body jerks while he sobs into the duct tape.

Then I do it again to his other leg. As I smile, a sick and twisted feeling of satisfaction comes over me when I see the blood run down his hairy legs.

I decide to hit both arms. I had to be quick with Nate because my life depended on it. But right now? I've got Colt and his friends here. I'm safe and can take my time.

Crying, he shakes his head, and I hit him in the stomach. My breathing picks up at how pathetic he looks. This was me—a sobbing mess on the floor—and it makes my teeth clench. How helpless I was. What would they have done to me if I hadn't killed Nate by the time Mike returned home?

I pull the trigger again on his hip. And then on his knee.

Finn reloads it for me twice. I pull the trigger over and over. Holding it up against Mike's body, he hangs there, head falling forward while I pump him full of nails. But he's not the one who's screaming, I am. Tears run down my face while my heart pounds in my chest. I don't let go until I run out again. Letting it drop to my side, Finn reaches out for it, but I step away from him, needing a moment.

"Princess." I blink tears away to see Colt now standing in front of me, and he reaches out his hand. "Hand me the nail gun."

I shake my head, too tired to go on but not ready to let go.

"It's empty again." He looks down at it dangling by my side, softly tapping my thigh. "He's dead. It's over."

I sniff, and his green eyes search mine. "You did good, princess." His warm hands cup my face, and I lick my wet lips. "How about we go home now?"

Yeah. That's what I need. Him and me in our bed. The world falls away when it's just us. He knows how to make nothing else matter.

I hold out the gun, and he takes it, handing it off to Finn.

Turning back to face me, Colt kisses me. His tongue invades my mouth, and I moan into his. My heavy arms wrap around his neck, and I open up for him, letting him dominate me.

One of his arms wraps around my back while his other hand holds my head in place. He growls deep in his chest when he tastes my tears.

I don't know what's going to happen today or tomorrow, but

I do know that no matter what, Colton Knox will be by my side, reminding me that he belongs to me. And I will crawl on my hands and knees, begging him to make me his.

The end

Thank you for taking the time to read Sabotage. I hope that you enjoyed it. Want to discuss Sabotage with other readers? Be sure to join the spoiler room on Facebook. Shantel Tessier's Spoiler Room. Please note that I have one spoiler room for all books, and you may come across spoilers from book(s) you have not had the chance to read yet. You must answer both questions in order to be approved.

Join spoiler room here: https://www.facebook.com/groups/246657056669108

If you want to see where it started for the Lords, please continue to read the prologue and chapter one of The Ritual: A Dark College Romance.

THE RITUAL

USA TODAY & WALL STREET JOURNAL BESTSELLING AUTHOR

SHANTEL TESSIER

Author's note:
The Ritual may contain triggers for some. As a reader, I find trigger warnings to be spoilers, but as an author, I understand that they are sometimes necessary. Although, I'm not going to list each one, (there are many) please feel free to email me at shanteltessierassistant@gmail.com with your specific trigger warning(s) and me or one of my assistants will let you know if that trigger is in the book.

For those of you who wish to go in blind; please remember this dark romance is a work of fiction, and I do NOT condone any situations or actions that take place between these characters.

PROLOGUE

L.O.R.D.

A LORD TAKES his oath seriously. Only blood will solidify their commitment to serve those who demand their complete devotion.

*He is a **Leader**, believes in **Order**, knows when to **Rule**, and is a **Deity**.*

A Lord must be initiated in order to become a member but can be removed at any time for any reason. If he makes it past the three trials of initiation, he will forever know power and wealth. But not all Lords are built the same. Some are stronger, smarter, hungrier than others.

*They are challenged just to see how far their **loyalty** will go.*

*They are pushed to their limits in order to prove their **devotion**.*

*They are willing to show their **commitment**.*

Nothing except their life will suffice.

Limits will be tested, and morals forgotten.

A Lord can be a judge, jury, and executioner. He holds power that is unmatched by anyone, other than his brother.

If they manage to complete all trials of initiation, he will be granted a reward—a chosen one. She is his gift for his servitude.

ONE

INITIATION

RYAT

Loyalty
Freshman year at Barrington University

I KNEEL IN the middle of the darkly lit room along with twenty other men. My hands are secured tightly behind my back with a pair of handcuffs. My shirt is torn, and blood drips from my busted lips. I'm panting, still trying to catch my breath while my heart beats like a drum in my chest. It's hard to hear over the blood rushing in my ears, and I'm sweating profusely.

We were dragged out of our beds in the middle of the night to serve. Our freshman classes at Barrington University start in two weeks, but we already have to show our loyalty to the Lords.

"You will always have to prove yourself," my father once told me.

"You were each given a task," the man calls out as he paces in front of us. His black combat boots slap against the concrete floor with each step, the sound echoing off the walls. "Kill or be killed. Now how many of you can fulfill it?"

"I can," I state, lifting my head to stick my chin out in the warm and sticky air. Sweat covers my brow after the fight. It's rigged. You are supposed to lose. The point is to wear you down. See just how much you have to give. How far you can go. I made sure to win mine. No matter what it took.

He smirks down at me like I'm fucking joking. "Ryat. You seem so confident in yourself."

"I know what I'm capable of handling," I say through gritted teeth. I don't like being second-guessed. We were each raised for this—to be a Lord.

Wealth got us here.

Yet our determination will separate us by the time it's over.

The man looks at the guy on my left and nods. The guy walks behind me and yanks me to stand by the back of my shirt. He undoes the cuffs, and I rip the shredded material up and over my head before dropping my hands to my sides when what I really want to do is rub my sore wrists.

Never show weakness. A Lord does not feel. He's a machine.

The man steps up to me with a knife in hand. He holds it out handle first to me, his black eyes almost glowing with excitement. "Show us what you can do."

Taking it from him, I walk over to the chair bolted to the floor. I yank the bloody sheet off the chair to reveal a man tied to it. His hands are cuffed behind his back, and his feet are spread wide and secured to the chair legs.

I'm not surprised I know him—he's a Lord. Or was. The fact that he's restrained tells me he's not anymore. But that doesn't change my orders.

Kill without questions.

You want to be powerful? Then you realize you are a threat to those who want your position. In order to succeed, you don't have to be stronger, just deadlier.

The man shakes his head, his brown eyes pleading with me to spare his life. Multiple layers of duct tape are placed over his mouth—those who spill secrets will be silenced. He thrashes in his chair.

Walking behind him, I look down at his cuffed wrists. He wears a ring on his right hand; it's a circle with three horizontal lines across the middle. It stands for power.

Not just anyone would know what it means, but I do. Because I wear the same one. Everyone in this room does. But just because you get one doesn't mean you'll keep it.

I reach down and grab his hand. He begins to shout behind the tape as he tries to fight me, but I remove the ring easily and walk back around to stand in front of him.

"You don't deserve this," I say to him, placing it in my pocket. "You betrayed us, your brothers, yourself. The payment for that is death."

When he throws his head back and screams into the tape, I press the knife to his neck, right below his jawline. His breathing fills the room, and his body strains, waiting for the first cut.

A Lord does not show mercy. Blood and tears are what we demand from those who betray us.

I press the tip of the knife into his neck, puncturing his skin enough for a thin line of blood to drip from the wound.

He begins to cry, tears running down his already bloody face.

"I uphold my duty. For I am a Lord. I know no boundaries when it comes to my servitude. I will obey, serve, and dominate," I recite our oath. "For my brother, I am a friend. I shall lay my life down for thee or take it." I stab the knife into his right thigh, forcing a muffled scream from his taped lips before yanking it out, letting the blood soak into his jeans while it drips off the end of the knife onto the concrete floor. "For we are what others wish to be." Circling him, I run the tip down his forearm, splitting the skin like I did his neck. "We will be held accountable for our actions." I stab him in the left thigh and tug it out as his sobbing continues. "For they represent who we truly are."

Jerking on the collar of his shirt, I rip it down the middle to expose his chest and stomach. The same crest that's on our rings is burned into his chest. It's what we are given once we pass our trials. Gripping the skin, I pull on it as far as I can with my right hand, then slide the blade through it with my left, cutting it from his body.

He sobs, snot flying out of his nose as the blood pours from the gaping hole in his skin. His body begins to shake while he fists his hands and thrashes in his chair. I throw the skin to the floor to rest at his feet. A souvenir for later.

I walk behind him. The only sound in the room is his cries muffled by the duct tape. I grab his hair, yanking his head back, and force his hips off the chair. His Adam's apple bobs when he swallows. I look down into his tear-filled eyes. "And you, my brother … are a traitor." Then I slice the blade across his neck, splitting it wide open. His body goes slack in the chair as the blood pours from the open wound like a waterfall, drenching his clothes instantly.

"Impressive." The man who handed me the knife begins to clap while silence now fills the room. Walking over to me, I throw the bloody knife up in the air, catching it by the tip of the blade and holding it out to him.

He comes to a stop and gives me a devious smile. "I knew you'd be one to watch." With that, he takes the knife, then turns and walks away.

I stand, still breathing heavily, now covered in not only my blood but a fellow brother's. Lifting my head, I look up at the two-way mirror on the second-floor balcony, knowing I'm being watched and knowing that I just passed my first test with flying colors.

The Ritual: A Dark College Romance is LIVE and FREE in KU

CONTACT ME

Shantel's Facebook Spoiler Room. Please note that I have one spoiler room for all books, and you may come across spoilers from book(s) you have not had the chance to read yet. You must answer both questions in order to be approved.

Join **Shantel Tessier's mailing list** for exclusive material and giveaways: https://bit.ly/37c1fEM

Facebook Reader Group: The Sinful side
Goodreads: Shantel Tessier
Instagram: shantel_tessierauthor
Website: Shanteltessier.com
Facebook Page: Shantel Tessier Author
TikTok: shantel_tessier_author

If you would like to join the street team or review team, please send all inquiries to shanteltessierassistant@gmail.com

Made in the USA
Middletown, DE
31 August 2024

60150975R00121